RETURN TO RACING

BOOKS BY W. E. BUTTERWORTH

AIR EVAC

CRAZY TO RACE

FAST AND SMART

FAST GREEN CAR

GRAND PRIX DRIVER

HELICOPTER PILOT

MARTY AND THE MICRO-MIDGETS

REDLINE 7100

ROAD RACER

SOLDIERS ON HORSEBACK

STOCK CAR RACER

THE WHEEL OF A FAST CAR

RETURN TO RACING

RETURN
to
RACING

by W. E. BUTTERWORTH

A W. W. NORTON BOOK
Published by
GROSSET & DUNLAP, INC.
New York

RETURN TO RACING

1

Ten days before, for what he devoutly hoped was the last time, Tony Fletcher, at home, had taken off his uniform. This was a uniform of tropical worsted, complete with Cap, Officer's, Company Grade, and Insignia, Metal, Officer's Grade of Rank, First Lieutenant, and Insignia, Metal, Qualification, Rated Army Aviator, and what was somewhat less formally known as fruit salad: The ribbons saying that he had been in the service, had been in Vietnam, had been wounded and that, in at least three incidences, his conduct had been above and beyond the call of duty. Tony had come home from Vietnam with a Distinguished Flying Cross, twenty-one Air Medals, a Bronze Star, and two Vietnamese medals for gallantry.

Wearing the ribbons had been something he'd done for his grandfather, who had been a professional soldier in another army, half a century before, across an ocean. Tony Fletcher felt a little uncomfortable as a certified hero and would have worn only his pilot's wings if it hadn't been for his grandfather.

The Old Man had wrapped him in a bear hug, then pushed him away to look proudly at the decorations on his chest, and then hugged him again.

"You have been true to your heritage," the Old Man said, and then, looking straight at Tony's father, "And you were an officer."

That wasn't exactly fair, Tony thought. His father, in his war, World War II, had been a First Sergeant. Grandfather Fletcher himself, before the name had been Americanized from Straylatworez to Fletcher, had been a Sergeant-Chef in the Czar's army.

His father didn't seem to mind the comparison. And Tony was honest enough with himself to be touched and pleased that his father and his grandfather were proud of him. He wore his uniform for three days, long enough to make a visit to Fletcher Trucking, long enough to wear it to church with his father and grandfather, long enough to be admitted to membership in his father's post of the Veterans of Foreign Wars of the United States; and then, ten days ago, the night he came home from the VFW, he took it off for what he hoped would be the last time.

For the next nine days, he wore what he thought of as civvies. He wore sports shirts and slacks most of the time, "civilian" khaki pants and shirt to take a turn behind the wheel of a cross-country 10-ton rig of Fletcher Trucking, just to keep his hand in, he said, but really because he liked to drive a big tractor trailer as a member in good standing of the Teamsters Union.

2

Today, in a hotel room in New York City, he put on what he thought of as another uniform. He was going back to work, and there was a uniform required for this, too.

It consisted of a pair of heavy-soled, highly polished black cordovan shoes. There were thigh-high woolen stockings, of a suitably subdued color. There was a narrow-shouldered, three-button, single-breasted suit from a clothing store which catered to three major Ivy League colleges and to the advertising business of New York City. Tony, who had gone to a very good but rather obscure state university, qualified for the suit, so to speak, because of his advertising affiliation.

He put on a white, button-down-collar shirt, an expensive regimental striped necktie and a narrow-brimmed summer hat.

He looked at himself in the mirror and decided there was more to the uniform business than a clever crack. He was dressed for the role he played, and there were subtle variations. He wasn't sure what he thought—most of it had developed while he was off at war—of the new styles, the Victorian double-breasted suits, the wide-knotted, bright neckties, the long hair styles, the slanted pockets, but he knew that even if he liked them, he couldn't wear them.

Anthony Fletcher was an account executive for Collier, Richards & Company, Advertising. (Specifically, he had been an account executive, and had been told that a job as such would be waiting for him when he returned from service. He was in fact, an account executive without an

3

account.) Account executives, like lawyers, doctors and life insurance salesmen, are supposed to give off an aura of calm, conservative competence. Tony had been around long enough to realize that while purple shirts and yellow ties and lace at the cuff might be perfectly all right for a copywriter, or an artist, or a photographer, account executives were supposed to look like—well, account executives.

He was, he decided, in the proper uniform to report for duty.

He was staying in a small hotel on East 50th Street. When he'd gone off to the army, he'd had a small apartment in a very nice building which, in his absence, had been torn down and replaced by a very large, very modern building which seemed to be constructed solely of steel girders and plate glass. He would have to find a new apartment, and from what he'd seen in last night's paper, that was going to be both difficult and expensive.

There was one pleasant ray of light there, however. In Vietnam, an officer who spent many hours reading the small print of Army Regulations had turned up one which said the army would pay the storage bill for the furniture Tony had put in storage when he'd gone in the army. The reasoning was that since he couldn't take his books and couches and bed and high-fi equipment with him to Vietnam, the army should take care of it for him.

Tony Fletcher walked out of his hotel and toward midtown Manhattan. He had breakfast in the ground-floor cafeteria of the Waldorf-Astoria, because he remembered that, despite the elegance the name implied, it was a fine, and reasonable, place to have breakfast.

While he was no longer a growing boy, he was inarguably a large male animal. He had ham and eggs and pancakes, a large glass of milk, a small glass of orange juice, and three cups of coffee.

Then he walked over to Park Avenue and along it and into the familar glass and marble lobby of the building in which Collier, Richards & Company occupied three whole floors.

He pushed the button which would stop the elevator at the 22nd floor. This was the upper of the floors occupied by Collier, Richards & Company, the floor occupied by the upper echelons of Collier, Richards & Company brass. He corrected himself, reminding himself that brass was an army word, and he was no longer in the army. Occupied by upper-level Collier, Richards & Company *executives*.

Shortly before going into the service, Tony himself had, literally, moved up to the 22nd floor. His office there, a cubicle just about large enough for his desk and an extra chair and a filing cabinet was not, in truth, as large as his office had been on the 19th floor when he'd been a copywriter. On the nineteenth floor, too, he'd had a window overlooking Park Avenue. On the 22nd floor, he'd had a splendid view of an elevator shaft in the building across the street, but he was on the 22nd floor, and that was supposed to be payment, in status, enough.

The door closed and the elevator moved upward. It

gave him a funny, remembered feeling in the pit of his stomach, and he thought two things: First, that this was the first elevator he'd been on since he went off to the army, and that it was far below the dignity of an old chopper pilot to get tipsy-tummy on an elevator.

The door whooshed open and he stepped out. He had, he thought, with some chagrin, gotten off at the wrong floor. This didn't look at all familiar. He turned to get back on the elevator. The door closed in his face.

"May I help you?" a bright, pleasant female voice inquired.

"I was looking for the 22nd floor," he said, feeling rather foolish.

"You've found it," she said, and that made him feel even more foolish.

"Collier, Richards & Company?" he asked.

"What department were you looking for?"

"I was looking for Mr. James," he said. He had almost said "Skeezix James," and that would have been an error. In these somewhat hallowed precincts, one did not refer to the vice-president, Creativity, by his nickname.

"I see," she said. "Do you have an appointment?"

"Well, he more or less expects me," Tony said. "I— work here. Or I used to."

"I see," she said with a polite smile, a distant smile, one even tinged with a little concern. If he worked here, how come he didn't know where he was?

"Is his office still down there?" Tony asked, pointing toward a door in an oak-paneled wall, and in the same moment walking toward it.

6

"Sir," the girl said, and Tony ignored her, embarrassed. He would find Skeezix' office without any further encounter with her.

He grasped the knob and turned and the door remained firmly shut.

"I'll have to announce you," the receptionist said, getting to her feet behind her very modern desk. "I'm not sure Mr. James has come in. May I have your name, please?"

"Tony Fletcher," he said. "Just tell his secretary, Tony Fletcher."

He stayed by the door, waiting for it to be opened. He thought of Skeezix' secretary, Mrs. Haas. Fine lady. She'd sent him a biweekly newsy letter when he was off in the army. If Skeezix wasn't in yet, there would be at least a cup of coffee and some pleasant, welcoming conversation until he showed up.

"Mr. Fletcher?" the receptionist said, and when he looked at her, she beckoned to him with her finger, and when he walked over to the desk, she handed him the telephone.

"This is Mr. James's secretary," a voice—not that of Mrs. Haas—said. "How may I help you, Mr. Fletcher?"

"I want to see Mr. James," he said.

"I wonder if you'd be good enough to tell me the nature of your business?" the secretary said. "Mr. James's schedule is quite busy today, and I'm not sure if I'll be able to fit you in."

"When do you expect him?" Tony countered.

"I'm not sure," she said, and Tony translated that

7

instantly: "If I knew, buddy, I wouldn't tell you."

"Would you please leave a note for Mr. James, saying that Mr. Fletcher is in the shop, and will try to see him later?" he said.

"Would you spell that, please?" the secretary asked.

When he hung up, he looked at the receptionist, who was still smiling uneasily at him, as if he were liable to do something outrageous, and asked:

"Is the personnel department still on the 21st floor?"

"Twentieth floor," she said. "Two floors down."

"Thank you," he said, and went and pushed the button for the elevator, wondering if his ears and neck were really red, or if they just felt that way.

Even the personnel office had changed. It now looked, Tony thought somewhat disagreeably, like the Small Loan Department of a bank, with glass-walled cubicles exposing people to the view of passers-by.

There was a blonde, almost a carbon copy of the one upstairs, behind another receptionist's desk.

"Good morning," she said, with a practiced smile.

"Good morning," Tony said. "Is Mr. Hobbel in, please? My name is Fletcher."

"Oh, I'm so sorry, but Mr. Hobbel has been transferred to San Francisco."

"Oh."

"Could anyone else help you?"

Tony searched his memory, unsuccessfully, for the name of someone else he knew in the personnel department.

"You are," she said, with what she must have thought

8

was tact, "interested in a position with Collier, Richards & Company?"

"Yes, I am," Tony said.

She handed him a five-by-seven-inch cardboard form. "If you'll just fill this out, I'll have someone see you."

It was a PRELIMINARY APPLICATION FOR EMPLOYMENT form.

"I used to work here," Tony said. "Do I have to fill this out?"

On the telephone from San Francisco, when he'd called Skeezix to tell him he was home, Skeezix had said: "I'll have a pencil sharpened and a chair warmed. Come home, fly-boy, we've missed you."

"Of course," she said. "It's procedure."

Tony had learned in the army that it is far easier to go along with "procedure" than to try to get out of it. He sat down at a small desk and filled out the form. About half-way through it, it was too much. He didn't fill it out as an applicant for employment would be expected to fill it out. For example, there was a blank which asked: "WHY DO YOU SEEK EMPLOYMENT WITH COLLIER, RICHARDS & COMPANY?"

Tony wrote: *I have this habit of eating*.

Another blank asked: "WHERE DID YOU FIRST HEAR OF COLLIER, RICHARDS & COMPANY?" and Tony replied: *Hear what?*

And in the blank where it asked, SALARY EXPECTED? he wrote: *"As much as I can get."*

When he turned it in, the receptionist looked at it,

9

arched her eyebrows, looked askance at him, and said, "Well, *really.*"

She got up, disapproval in her stance and walk, and disappeared into one of the glass cubicles. After a moment, she came out, held the door open, and said:

"Mr. Fletcher."

He walked to the cubicle. He had not, despite the glass wall, been able to see the occupant of the cubicle. It was still another blonde, this one with her hair done up—he searched for the word and found it—*severely,* parted in the middle and wound up in sort of a bun on either side of her head. She wore very large, red-rimmed, circular glasses. Nevertheless, she was a looker.

It was immediately evident that she didn't think very much of the wit of Tony Fletcher.

"Good morning," she said, like a schoolteacher. "Perhaps you'll explain this?"

The receptionist stood by the door eavesdropping. Tony felt like a fool, but the receptionist annoyed him. He turned and glowered at her until she closed the door.

"Who are you?" Tony asked the blonde behind the glasses and the desk.

"I'm Miss Chedister," she said.

"Miss Chedister," Tony said. "I'm Anthony Fletcher, returning to the firm after military service."

"Oh," she said. "You should have said so." She pushed a button on her intercom, and said: "Mary, would you please bring me the folder on Mr. Fletcher, Anthony? It should be in the inactive file." She turned back to Tony and said, "Please have a seat."

"Thank you," Tony said.

He looked at her and she looked at him, and then away. They had stopped being a seeker-of-employment and the possible-giver-of-same. She was a good-looking blonde and he was a tall, black-haired, deeply tanned young man in an expensive suit and sure of himself.

The blonde appeared at the door to the cubicle, knocked, was told to come in, and then announced: "Miss Chedister, I can't find any file—"

"Are you sure?" Miss Chedister asked.

"Oh, come on," Tony said. "Eff Ell Eee Tea See Haitch Eee Are, Anthony."

"I looked through the whole file," the blonde said righteously. "There is *no* folder on you, Mr. Fletcher."

There was a discreet buzzing outside which only after a minute Tony recognized as a telephone ringing. The blonde went to answer it. The blonde behind the glasses and the desk said:

"Mr. Fletcher, if this is some sort of a joke, I must tell you, the point is lost on me."

"I was the account executive for Blackman Boats," Tony said. "And before that, I was chief copywriter for Corey Rubber Company. If you don't have my name in the files out there, Miss Chedister, your files are in lousy shape."

"You look awfully young to have been an account executive," she said, not very pleasantly, and he countered in kind:

"And you look a little young to be playing executive," he said.

11

She flushed, and in that moment, her telephone buzzed.

"Personnel, Miss Chedister," she said, obviously relieved to have something to do besides spar with Tony. "Oh, good morning. Just fine, thank you. Is there something I can do for you?" There was a pause, a look of disbelief, and then she said, "Why, yes, he is." She handed the telephone to Tony.

"Hello, you ugly Russian airplane driver," Skeezix James said. His voice was loud enough to carry through the small cubicle.

"Hello, Skeezix," Tony said, very much relieved to hear his voice.

"When I got the message, I knew just where to find you," James said.

"How?"

"Decide where the best-looking blonde in the shop is, and there you find the Mad Russian. It's as simple as that."

The blonde behind the glasses flushed and then, nervously, took them off.

"I don't work here, you know," Tony said. "I don't even exist. They don't have my records."

"I've got your file up here," Skeezix said. "Come on up, and I'll even buy you a cup of coffee."

"Leave a pass to the fortress," Tony said. "The last time I was up there, I couldn't get past the exterior guard."

"I'll lower the drawbridge," Skeezix James said. "Come on up."

12

Tony put down the phone and smiled broadly at Miss Chedister.

"Thanks for the warm welcome," he said. "It's always nice to know you're loved."

"Welcome back to Collier, Richards and Company, Mr. Fletcher," she said, and her face was almost, if not quite, as red as the red rims of her glasses.

2

When Tony had gone off into the army, Skeezix James customarily had worn clothing very much like what Tony was now wearing. The first thing Tony saw when he was shown into James's office was that that had changed. James came around his desk to shake Tony's hand wearing a double-breasted, six-button, powder-blue jacket, yellowish glen plaid trousers, a shirt of approximately the same hue, and a very wide, wide-knotted polka-dot tie. The effect was startling.

"How are you, Tony?" James said, genuinely glad to see him, wringing his hand. "It's good to have you back."

"It's good to be back," Tony said, and then the words popped out of his mouth. "I see you've changed tailors."

"Throughout nature," James said, smiling but quite serious, "the male of the species normally has the more colorful plumage. Why should homo sapiens be different?"

"I guess I'm just used to army green," Tony said.

14

"I sort of hoped you would show up in your uniform," James said. "It would have made a better picture."

"What do you mean by that?"

The question was answered by the intercom. "Mr. Kelp is here, Mr. James," it said.

"Send him in," James said.

Mr. Kelp, when he came through the door, apparently had the same tailor as Skeezix James. Three years ago, Tony thought, he would have thought they were dressed up for some sort of a costume party.

"Jack, this is Tony Fletcher," James said, and Kelp shook Tony's hand.

"Welcome home," he said. "We've been expecting you." He handed James a sheet of paper. "I hope this is all right."

James read it, and then handed it to Tony. "Check that over, Tony, and see if we left anything out." To Kelp, he said: "How quickly can we get a picture of him?"

"An hour after he appears in photo," Kelp said.

"You'd better send pics with it," James said, and then looked at Tony, who was, with some embarrassment, reading what the paper said:

Collier, Richards & Company
Advertising
390 Park Avenue, New York

FOR IMMEDIATE RELEASE:
Further Information: John Kelp
MU 9-5879

15

TO: *Advertising Age*
    The New York Times

Anthony Fletcher, former Blackman Boats Company account executive, returned to Collier, Richards & Company today from distinguished service in Vietnam.

Fletcher, 24, had been Collier, Richards & Company's youngest account executive, and one of the youngest—if not the youngest—in the industry before entering the army. He joined the firm after college, and rose rapidly from trainee to copywriter to chief copywriter for Corey Rubber, Inc., before being named to the Blackman account.

His rise in the service was equally meteoric. Drafted as a private, he was commissioned as an infantry lieutenant on graduation from flight school, and sent immediately to Vietnam. After initial service as a pilot of cargo helicopters, he was given command of a section of helicopter gunships. Shortly after having been awarded the Distinguished Flying Cross, he was promoted to First Lieutenant.

Fletcher was also decorated with the Bronze Star and the Air Medal with twenty clusters for subsequent awards, and with two decorations for valor in action from the Vietnamese government.

Pending specific assignment, he will be a member of the Collier, Richards & Company Research and Creativity Committee. Fletcher, a bachelor, is the son of Peter Fletcher, President of Fletcher Trucking Corporation.

The subject of the press release said a word which, fairly common in Vietnam, was not the sort of word one used around Collier, Richards & Company.

"Tony," Skeezix James said. "Am I going to have to wash out your mouth with soap?"

"Sorry," Tony said. "But what do you have to do this for?"

"An up-and-coming pillar of the advertising community questioning the value of advertising? That's a worse sin than bad words, sport," James said.

"You know what I mean," Tony said.

"It's what they call public relations, Tony," James said. "The firm is basking in your reflected glory."

Tony almost said the word again, but stopped himself in time.

"Besides," James said, unabashed, "I thought that Jack did you a real good turn, personally."

"How?" Tony asked.

"That last sentence, where it says you're a bachelor and the son of the Fletcher Trucking Company. If that doesn't get you invitations to all sorts of dances, dinners and parties, I'll be very surprised. Rich, heroic bachelors are in short supply here."

"I'm not rich and I'm not a hero," Tony said.

James didn't reply. He just raised an eyebrow and looked at Tony, waiting for Tony to realize that the sentence was true. The Fletcher Trucking Company, begun by his father with a couple of surplus World War II army trucks was now a very large and very successful trucking operation. With the exception of stock held by Tony's grandfather, and stock he had been given, his father owned it outright. While the only money Tony had ever taken from the company was wages for driving a truck, that did not alter the fact that his stock in it was worth a great deal of money, and that he would—because he was the only son and grandson—eventually wind up with just about all of it.

And while he didn't feel at all heroic, he realized that the army, when they pinned the medals on him, had certified him as a hero.

"I still don't like it," he said lamely. "Do you have to do it?"

"Yes, I think we do," James said. "You're wrong about this, Tony," he added, and the implication was there: I may not be right, but I *am* the boss.

"What's this Research and Creativity Committee?" Tony asked, slightly ashamed that he was backing down and changing the subject.

"At the moment," James said, "It consists of the two most brilliant members of the company team. You and me."

"What is it—what are we—supposed to do?"

"Well, we'll have lunch together from time to time, and discuss baseball and the ladies. To get right to the point, Tony, while there is no question in anyone's mind that we're glad to have you back, and that your future lies with the firm, the cold truth is that, for the moment, we don't have any idea what to do with you."

"I don't get Blackman back?"

"We've had someone doing Blackman for two years and nine months, Tony. Blackman is satisfied with him, and it would be sort of dirty pool to move the guy out."

"And Corey?"

"We're paying you too much money to write copy for Corey," James said. "Now, just to make myself clear, you will, of course, sit in on the think-tank sessions of both accounts. Blackman would want that, Corey would want that, and there is no question in anyone's mind about your past contributions to those accounts. We're not putting you down, in other words, but just looking for the slot to push you up into. Which sounds like a split infinitive."

"Oh," Tony said.

James was now conciliatory and charming. Tony felt that he was being sold something.

"Relax, Tony," James said. "Go get your picture taken, go see the charming, red-rimmed Miss Chedister and get your paperwork straightened out, and then get yourself settled in town. Go find an apartment. Get used to sidewalks and inside plumbing, and then come to work. Say next Monday."

Skeezix was smiling at him broadly, half-fatherly, half like a buddy. But he hadn't been making suggestions, he'd been giving orders.

"Yes, sir," Tony said, tempering the sarcasm with a smile. "I'll see you next Monday."

"Get yourself some new threads, Tony," Skeezix said. "You look like an undertaker."

19

"I feel like one," Tony said. "You don't mind if I come to work like this, do you?"

"Not at all," James said. "Good to see you, Tony."

The interview was closed.

"This won't take a minute, Mr. Fletcher," Kelp said. "I've got a photographer standing by in photo."

When he'd gone off to the army, the only person in the company who had called him "Mr. Fletcher" was the young secretary he'd shared with two other men, and even she had forgotten that respectful form of address very frequently. This fellow Kelp meant it. Tony realized suddenly that this was like being commissioned. One moment, you're a nice guy, with a first name, and the next you're an officer and a gentleman, with a title.

Around here he was no longer to be "Tony, the Boy Wonder of Blackman Boats" but "Mr. Fletcher."

He wasn't entirely sure that he was going to like it.

He posed for his picture, and the photographer, too, called him "Mr. Fletcher." And then he went to the personnel office again, and the blonde receptionist who had given him trouble stopped him and said:

"Mr. Fletcher, I'm sorry about what happened before. You have to understand that I just didn't think that Mr. James himself would come get your file from the files. I hope there's no hard feelings?"

"Of course not," Tony said.

And Miss Chedister spoke to him, too: "I hope you haven't formed the idea that we're normally as sloppy as it looked around here, Mr. Fletcher," she said. "I looked into it. First of all, your file wasn't with the other employee-

20

inactive folders. It was kept with the active executive files, and then, of course, Mr. James came down here himself yesterday and got it."

"Forget it," Tony said.

There were a surprising number of forms for him to sign, and then she began to hand him things.

"This is your temporary after-hours admission pass, Mr. Fletcher," she said. "We'll have a regular identity card, with your photograph, within a couple of days."

"What's it for?"

"So you can come in the office at night and on week-ends," she said.

"Oh."

"And here is your key."

"What's it open?"

"The door to the executive wing," she said. "And the executive washroom."

"My, how mighty the lowly have risen," he said. "I get to use the executive john, do I?"

"Why, yes, of course," she said.

"Maybe I ought to go buy myself a Homburg and a cane," he said.

There was the suggestion of a smile on her lips, and then she went on.

"The records show that you've kept your American Express and other credit cards active while you were in the service?"

"That's right."

"Well, we'll just notify them to bill the company from now on," she said.

"All right."

"Would you like a cash advance for expenses?"

"No, thank you," he said.

"If you need money, just go to Miss Kelly and sign a chit."

"Thank you," he said.

"I think that's all, Mr. Fletcher," she said. "Thank you for being so patient with us."

"When I come to work on Monday," he said. "Where do I go?"

"We'll have an office set up for you by then," she said.

"Does your splendid service end at five o'clock?" Tony asked.

"I don't think I follow you," she said.

"Well, I was thinking that maybe you'd be willing to have dinner with a new boy in town," he said.

She looked at him to see if he was serious, and then she put him down.

"I'm sorry, Mr. Fletcher," she said. "I don't think that would be a good idea."

His temper flared just a moment. "I'm really a very nice guy, Miss Chedister," he said. "You ought to read the press release they're sending out."

"I just think that one's private and professional life should be separate," she said.

"You're probably right," he said. "I have a tendency to think the whole rest of the world is out of step with me."

Two hours and ten minutes after he had entered the building, he went out of it again. He would not be expected back, he realized, for a full week. He corrected that. He would not be welcome for a full week.

He walked back to his hotel, bought a newspaper in the lobby and went to his room. He took off his suit and the expensive shoes and his necktie, and put on a pair of khaki pants and a pair of suede, gum-soled shoes. He went over the listings of available apartments, and circled those that looked promising.

Then he went apartment hunting, absolutely convinced that it was going to be a long and difficult process, and probably would entail more hiking through Manhattan's stone corridors than he'd ever done in the army.

By the time darkness fell, he was pretty discouraged. He had been shown absolutely unsuitable apartments, the size of a large closet, at a price he thought he could afford, and he had been shown unsuitable apartments, only slightly larger, at prices he absolutely couldn't afford. He was uptown by then, in what is known as Yorkville, the German section.

He passed a small, step-down restaurant in the basement of a brownstone building. There was a small sign, THE GOLDEN SAMOVAR, and he remembered then that he hadn't had any lunch. He turned and went down the stairs and went inside.

The headwaiter took one look at him and registered disapproval on his face.

"All I want is a cup of tea," Tony said, remembering that he was wearing the khakis and the tieless shirt.

"This way, please," the headwaiter said, with a shrug of

23

his shoulders that made it quite plain it would be easier to serve the bum a cup of tea than to argue about standards of proper dress.

After a long delay, the waiter appeared with a cup and saucer. The cup was full of a very pale, lukewarm liquid.

"Russian tea," the waiter said, with the clear implication that Tony wouldn't like it, and moved quickly away.

The tea tasted as bad as it looked. Tony took two sips, decided against walking out in a rage, which was what the waiter obviously hoped he would do, and waited for him to come close again. When he did, Tony called:

"This tea didn't come out of a samovar."

"I beg your pardon?" the waiter replied, outraged dignity in every syllable.

"This tea didn't come out of a samovar," Tony repeated, but this time in Russian. The waiter's eyes widened.

"You speak Russian," he said, quite unnecessarily.

"As well as you speak English," Tony said, in Russian. "Now please bring me some tea, and I have changed my mind, and want a menu."

"You should have said something when you came in," the waiter said, in Russian, and frowning disapproval now, more than ever, snatched the cup and saucer from the table. He disappeared through swinging, portholed doors into what was obviously the kitchen, and before he came back, Tony became aware that heads peered through the portholes at him.

When he did come back, he was followed by a very

large, black-haired, muscular young man in chef's whites who looked very much like Tony Fletcher.

"Here you are, sir," the waiter said icily.

It was Russian tea, and Tony said so. "Much better," he said.

"I'm glad you like it, sir," the muscular young man said sarcastically, and in Russian.

"How do you guys make any money," Tony asked, in English, "treating the customers as if they've got leprosy, or something?"

"I gather you haven't been in New York long, sir," the muscular young man said, in Russian.

"That's right, how can you tell?"

"We get very little," the muscular young man said, in Russian, "of what we Americans call repeat business from the members of the Soviet Mission to the UN."

"Is that what you think I am? A Russian-Russian?" Tony asked.

"You're a Russian," the young man said. "You didn't learn that dialect at the Army Language School."

"No, but I almost wound up teaching out there," Tony said, now in English, and then switching, jokingly, to a high-toned Russian, "Permit me to introduce myself, Anthony Fletcher, formerly Straylatworez, late lieutenant, infantry, United States Army."

The muscular young man's eyes widened and smiled, and he switched to English. "Buddy, you had me fooled, and him, too. First you were a beatnik, and then a communist, and we don't like either in here."

"I'm not either one, can I stay?" Tony said.

25

"The Restaurant Golden Samovar welcomes its distinguished guest," the muscular young man said formally, and then sat down. He turned to the waiter. "Get us something to munch on," he said, "and get us a bottle of vodka. *American* vodka." He turned to Tony. "By way of apology."

"I accept," Tony said. "I think I've earned a drink. I've walked all over Manhattan today, and with absolutely no success."

"Looking for a job?"

"I've got a job. I'm looking for someplace to live."

"That's a shame. Russian-speaking waiters are getting harder and harder to find," the young man said. "Pretty good money in it, if you don't like what you're doing?"

"Maybe I would, after a while," Tony said. "But not right now. You don't happen to know where I could find an apartment, do you?"

"I don't," the muscular young man said, after a moment's thought. "But after we have a drink and a little to eat, I'll call Uncle Pieter. He will probably know."

The bottle of vodka was served cold, chilled like a bottle of wine, and on a tray with heavy, very dark bread and a dish of horseradish. It was just like home for Tony; his grandfather always drank this way. A piece of bread was torn off, heaped with horseradish, and put in the mouth. Then a large sip of the vodka. It wasn't what could be called a delicate taste, but it was a memorable one.

"You're from a Russian family," the young man said, then remembered: "I haven't introduced myself. I'm Leo

26

—Leopold—Orlovsky. My mother and I own this place. It was my father's."

They shook hands. "What I said before, about the Language School?" Orlovsky said. "The minute I got out of college and into the army, right back to the classroom! I taught out there for two years. I would rather have gone to Vietnam."

"I went to Vietnam," Tony said. "I would rather have taught Russian."

They laughed, and then Orlovsky returned to his original subject.

"You ever wait on tables?"

"When I was in college," Tony said. "For three months. I hated it."

"I hate it, too," Leo said. "But somebody has to do it. Better you than me."

"What's that supposed to mean?"

"I'll guarantee you thirty-five bucks," Orlovsky said. "If you don't make that in tips, I'll make up the difference. You make more than that, it's yours."

"I think you're serious," Tony said.

"This place starts getting packed in about thirty minutes," Leo said. "We've got a good restaurant. Plus, you've got tasting privileges in the kitchen. We quit at about 11:30. It's not bad money, you know."

"What am I supposed to wear, my beatnik suit?" Tony said. It was crazy, but he really could think of no good reason why he should not wait on tables. It seemed far more attractive a proposition than going back to his hotel, or going alone to the movies.

"I've got waiters' suits in the back," Orlovsky said. "How about it?"

"Why not?" Tony said.

"And Uncle Pieter will be in, and we'll see about finding you an apartment. Where are you now?"

"In a hotel," Tony said.

"You can't keep that up for long, the prices they charge," Orlovsky said. "Come on, let's go, before you start scaring away the paying customers."

3

Leo Orlovsky made a few quick telephone calls to fix things with the waiter's union, and then he outfitted Tony with a waiter's uniform. It consisted of a well-worn, long-tailed waiter's frock coat, a dickey, complete with tie from the Mid-Manhattan Restaurant Uniform Supply Company, a pair of worn pants which had to be pinned up at the cuffs and tight around Tony's waist, and an order pad.

"You're a natural, Boris," Orlovsky said. "Can you fake an accent?"

"Vat sort of aan haccent vould you like?" Tony said, and they both laughed. "What's with the Boris business?" Tony asked, and Orlovsky pointed to a pin on the frock coat. "YOUR WAITER IS BORIS," it read.

"OK," Tony said.

"You understand the menu?" Orlovsky asked, and handed one to Tony. He knew most of the dishes, and Orlovsky explained the rest.

29

"You've got five tables in the back," Orlovsky said. "They're closest to the kitchen. The man whose place you're taking is old, and we try to make it easier for him. And then when I fill in for him, I pull rank. The boss gets the shortest walk."

"OK," Tony said. "But with me as a waiter, you may not be in the restaurant business tomorrow."

"I'll take my chances."

Leo Orlovsky was right. Once the customers started coming in, they came in steadily. By seven-thirty, they were clustered deeply around the bar, waiting for tables. They seemed to be divided into one-fourth Eastern Europeans of one form or another, and three-fourths just regular people who liked either the Russian food, or the quartet of gypsy violinists, or both.

It was crowded, and Tony had no trouble with serving: Any way he could get the food onto the table without spilling it in someone's lap was considered proper service.

By quarter to ten, he was tired, for it was harder work than it appeared to be at first sight. And by then, he knew that he was going to make more money on tips than the thirty-five dollars Leo had guaranteed him. Leo was also going to lose money on the tasting privileges he had given Tony. Tony had eaten steadily during his trips into the kitchen. The Golden Samovar, in Tony's opinion, put out a splendid *Szekelygulas*, or Transylvanian Goulash, and a superb *blini*. This was a sort of small, unsweetened pancake folded over a teaspoon of caviar. He had managed to pop one of those into his mouth a number of times while waiting for his orders to be prepared.

30

At about ten-fifteen, disaster loomed. When he peered through the porthole to the restaurant, he saw the head-waiter ceremoniously ushering to one of his tables a tall, hawk-faced character in an Ivy League suit, and a tall, good-looking blonde wearing red-rimmed glasses, who spent her business day in the personnel department of Collier, Richards & Company.

"Uh oh," Tony said.

"Something wrong, Tony?" Leo asked at his side.

"No," Tony said, and chuckled. "I don't think so, when I think about it."

He pushed open the door and went to the table.

"Good evening," he said, with the fake accent, "m"sieu and madame. How nice to see you again, Miss Chedister."

Her eyes opened. "Fletcher!" she said.

"Boris Straylatworez at your service, madame," Tony said, adding, "and sir."

"I didn't know you knew this place," the man said.

"I've been here once or twice before," Miss Chedister said.

"Madame graces our humble restaurant," Tony said. "And now, how may I serve you? A cocktail, perhaps?"

"I think that's a good idea, Boris," the man said. "What do you recommend?"

"I don't think you and the gracious lady would like the Russian vodka, sir—" Tony said, and, as Tony thought he would, the man bit.

"Why not?" he said. "This is a Russian restaurant. We came here for Russian food. Let's go whole hog."

31

"If you insist, sir," Tony said. "And may I recommend the *blini* for an hors d'oeuvre?"

"What's a blini, Boris?" Miss Chedister asked.

"Trust me, madame," Tony said.

"All right," she said, somewhat doubtfully, and smiled.

"And for the entrée, may I suggest *Töltött Hunyady Rostelyos?*"

"What is it?" the man asked. "I don't think I know that particular Russian dish."

"It is a steak dish," Tony said. "With Hungarian overtones."

Miss Chedister's eyes went even wider.

"That sounds fine," the man said. "We'll try that, if that's all right with you, Barbara?"

So Barbara's her name. Splendid name. Fits like a glove. I wonder where she got this jerk.

"And we'll consider a sweet a little later, shall we?" Tony said.

"I think that's a good idea, Boris," the young man said.

"Boris!" Miss Chedister—Barbara—said.

"Yes, gracious lady?" Tony asked, straight-faced.

"Nothing, nothing," she said, and began to search in her purse.

"And you're sure, sir, you would like the Vodka *à la Russe?*" Tony said.

"Certainly," the young man said. "I've told you twice already, Boris."

"Your wish is my command," Tony said, and bowed away from the table. Barbara was suddenly struck by a fit of coughing. Or at least, she made gasping noises and buried her flushed face in her handkerchief.

Tony went to the kitchen, placed the order, "tasted" another blini, and then set up the vodka tray. He went out to their table and placed it before them with a flourish. He could tell from the look on the man's face that Barbara had not spilled the beans. Probably, he thought, because she wasn't quite sure what beans to spill.

"It comes with bread?" the man asked.

"And what you Americans call horseradish," Tony said.

"Is it hot? How do you do it, anyway?"

"Would m'sieu permit me to demonstrate?"

"By all means, Boris," the man said grandly.

Tony winked at Barbara and shook his head "no" pointing to the tray as he bent over it. She looked at him in utter confusion. Tony tore off a small piece of the dark bread, heaped it very liberally with horseradish and then put an ounce of vodka into a glass. He put the whole in his mouth, added the vodka, and with a great deal of effort, managed to keep a straight face until the sensation passed.

"That's obviously not very hot horseradish," the man said.

"On the contrary, sir," Tony said, surprised to find that he could talk. "That is very strong horseradish."

"Not, Boris, to an old horseradish addict," the man said, heaping the horseradish on a piece of bread.

"If I may be so bold to suggest, m'sieu, that one might well go slowly, the first time—" Tony said.

33

He got a look of tolerant superiority in reply. The bread and horseradish were popped into the man's mouth, and then the jigger of vodka. His face turned red, and seemed for a moment to be paralyzed. Then, from each eye, tears ran down his face. After a very long moment, he said: "Delicious." It came out like steam from a leaking radiator. "Just delicious."

"None for me, thank you," Barbara Chedister said. "That's too strong for me."

"Nonsense," the man said. He had control of his voice again, and he'd discreetly wiped the tear tracks from his cheeks with the napkin. His masculinity was in question, and he rose to the challenge. He reached for more bread and spooned out more horseradish. Tony almost felt sorry for him.

Someone called "Boris" behind him, and he had to tend to other customers. He was aware that Barbara Chedister's eyes were on him, and for that reason, he put on as many professional waiter's airs as he could. He even took the risk of balancing a tray on one hand over his shoulder, a standard waiter's trick that he had once before tried to do, and failed, and sent $13.45 worth of china crashing to the floor of the Student Union Cafeteria.

This time it worked, and he was pretty smug about his success. Barbara enjoyed, as he thought she would, the blinis and the beaten steak with green peppers and onions and ham and sour cream that made up into *Töltött Hunyady Rostelyos*. Both she and her date said there was no room left for dessert.

When they left, her date paid with a credit card, and

instead of the customary fifteen per cent, he had written, "Tip, 10%." Tony wondered whether he was just a cheapskate or whether he sensed what Tony had done to him with the horseradish and vodka.

"I hope madame will grace our restaurant with her beauty and charm soon again," Tony said, bowing deeply. "And m'sieu, too, of course."

"Thank you very much, Boris," Barbara Chedister said, and shook her head in bewilderment and left.

About half-past eleven, as quickly as it had built up, business dropped off. The last customers at Tony's five tables were gone before midnight. He went into the kitchen and took off the dickey and had a cup of coffee, and, just because there seemed to be a little batter left over in the bowl, fried himself a couple of blinis.

He had made, for five hours work, and including the gracious 10% from Barbara's date, just over fifty dollars. He thought, too, that he'd earned every nickel of it. He was worn out.

"I got you a temporary permit from the waiter's union," Leo Orlovsky said. "It's good for a week, and I'll pay the dues. If you want to keep working, I'll split the cost of regular entrance fees with you."

"Not for me, thank you," Tony said. "The one thing that this night's work has done for me is to make me grateful for my regular job."

"I didn't think about that, Tony," Orlovsky said. "What time do you have to go to work in the morning?"

"I don't go to work until next Monday," Tony said.

"Good. Uncle Pieter thinks he may have a place for

35

you, and you can look at it tomorrow, and then come in for the lunch trade."

"Oh, come on, Leo. I told you I don't want a steady job doing this."

"You need an apartment, and I need a waiter. Trust me, *Tovarich*," he said, "and I'll make it worth your while."

It was entirely possible, Tony thought, that now that she knew where he worked, she just might drop in. Out of pure feminine curiosity.

"OK," he said.

"Come up here about ten in the morning," Leo said. "And Uncle Pieter will be waiting for you. I don't know what he's got in mind, and, maybe I shouldn't have, but I told him you'd go as high as two-fifty a month. Can you afford that much?"

"If you get me a decent place for that money, I'll wait tables until next Sunday," Tony said. "And I'll even pay for the food I steal from the kitchen."

"Next Sunday," Leo said. "We're closed on Sunday."

Uncle Pieter, the next morning, turned out to be a gentleman in his late seventies whose personality, if not his physique, was very much like Tony's grandfather. Grandfather Fletcher, like his son and grandson, was broad shouldered and big boned, and more or less heavy featured. Uncle Pieter, properly Pieter Pieterovich Orlovsky, probably weighed something around 110 pounds, and stood about five feet five. Like Grandfather Fletcher, he had a full head of heavy hair, silver gray, and, like Grandfather Fletcher, an aura of command and self-confidence, manifested by dramatic gestures that would have done either of them well if they had pursued a career on the stage.

Pieter Pieterovich Orlovsky, wearing (and it seemed perfectly appropriate for him) a Homburg, a double-breasted topcoat with a fur collar, and carrying a cane, led Tony back over to Fifth Avenue, and then down Fifth Avenue past what Tony knew was about the most expensive real estate anywhere in the world.

Richard Nixon had lived in one of these buildings, and Nelson Rockefeller had lived on a different level of floors.

Just past the building which at one time had simultaneously housed the governor of the State of New York and the President-Elect of the United States of America, Pieter Pieterovich Orlovsky directed Tony Fletcher into the lobby of a building which struck Tony as being just about as elegant, and probably just as expensive.

"In here?"

"You don't like it? Is there something wrong with it?" the old man asked, raising his voice and his eyebrows simultaneously.

"Can I afford it?"

"Trust me," the old man said grandly.

Outer and inner lobby doors were opened by uniformed doormen who apparently knew the old man, and literally bowed him inside. He stopped halfway through the lobby before a door which had a sign reading RESI-DENT MANAGER in gold letters.

He rapped, at once imperiously and gently, on the door with the handle of his cane. It was opened after a moment by another gentleman of advanced years and silver hair, this one about as large as Tony's grandfather. When he saw who had knocked, he smiled broadly, opened his arms wide, embraced Mr. Orlovsky and said, in Russian, that only that very morning his wife had given him firm orders to get in touch so that they could arrange a little dinner somewhere.

"I would present to you, my old friend, the former Lieutenant Anthony Straylatworez, who has Americanized his name to Fletcher," Mr. Orlovsky said.

The big man actually clicked his heels as he bowed and put out his hand.

"I am honored, Lieutenant," he said.

"I have mentioned your apartment to Lieutenant Fletcher," Mr. Orlovsky said. "Presuming it meets his needs, he may be willing to take it off your hands."

The big man's smile diminished, perceptibly, if just barely.

"Lieutenant Fletcher is just returned from fighting the communists," Mr. Orlovsky said. "He has just found employment in the city, and he needs a decent place to live."

"Would it be presumptuous of me, Lieutenant, to inquire as to the nature of your profession?" the big man asked.

"I'm in the advertising business," Tony said. "I work for Collier, Richards and Company."

"And may I ask what you do?"

"I don't know yet," Tony said. "I just got here, and I don't know what they're going to have me doing."

38

"He seems," the big man said, in Russian, "to be a young man of some dignity, breeding and education."

"Who also speaks fluent Russian," Mr. Orlovsky said.

The big man was not embarrassed. "That also speaks well for him," he said, in English. "Come, we'll see the apartment."

"Excuse me," Tony said. "I don't mean to be rude. But I don't think I could afford to live in an apartment building like this." He decided to make a joke. "My grandfather was a Sergeant-Chef in the Czar's army, not a Grand Duke in the Czar's court. I work for a living."

"My father," the big man said," on the other hand, *was* a Grand Duke. When he came to this country, he was given employment as the doorman of this building. I grew up in this building. There was once a grand lady who lived here. I used to earn pocket money by walking her dogs, and doing her other small services. When she died, she was gracious enough to bequeath to me the quarters occupied for long years by her chauffeur. They are somewhat less elegant than this address might suggest, but I feel they might prove adequate for a young man beginning his career in the city. Would you care to see them?"

"May I ask how much you're asking?"

"If you find them satisfactory," the big man said, "you would be my guest."

"I couldn't do that."

"Don't be so impetuous," the big man said. "We would have to reach a gentlemen's understanding that an appropriate contribution would be made each month to Saint

Sophia's Russian Orthodox Church." He paused. "That removes all sorts of unpleasant bureaucratic processes from the transaction."

"How much of a *contribution* would be appropriate?" Tony asked.

"Oh," he shrugged, "somewhere in the neighborhood of two hundred dollars. As I've said, the accommodations can hardly be termed luxurious. Would you care to see them?"

"Very much," Tony said.

They rode to the tenth floor in an oak-paneled elevator. The door opened on a small foyer. Five doors opened from the foyer. Three of them bore signs 10-A, 10-B and 10-C, obviously leading to apartments. The fourth read FIRE ESCAPE. The fifth was bare. The big man put a key in the lock and pushed the door open.

The apartment consisted of a tiny foyer, a kitchen the size of a large closet, a bedroom just slightly larger, and a large living-dining room with two windows, one overlooking Central Park and one around the corner, but also overlooking Central Park. It was almost too good to be true. It was precisely what Tony Fletcher knew he wanted, and knew he had no chance whatever of finding.

"It's a bit small," the big man said. "But rather light, for servants' quarters, and perhaps you might find it adequate."

"Yes, sir," Tony said. "I'd like to live here."

"It's agreed then," the big man said. "And I presume that two hundred dollars will be, once you get your feet on the ground, within your budget?"

40

"Yes, sir," Tony said, and then he felt obliged to add, "Sir, I don't want to travel under false colors. I've got a good job. I make pretty good money."

"Save it," the big man said. "You will soon find a young woman and get married. When that happens, you must understand, it will be necessary for you to find other accommodations. In the meantime, I hope you will be happy here."

"I'm sure I will be," Tony said.

"There is one telephone connected to the building switchboard," the big man said. "If you like, I'll arrange for a private line with the telephone company."

"That'd be fine," Tony said. "When could I move in?"

"Whenever you like," the big man said, and handed Tony the key, making sort of a ceremony of it. Tony thanked him, wrote out a check to Saint Sophia's Church, and they left. They made it back to the Golden Samovar just in time for Tony to put on his uniform and handle the first luncheon customers.

In the break between the late luncheon customers and the first of the early diners, he called the storage warehouse and arranged for his furniture to be delivered to his new apartment. It would, they told him, be delivered first thing in the morning.

Barbara Chedister didn't appear in the restaurant that night, but he looked for her anyway. On his second day as a waiter, he made $61.80 in tips, and took some pride in the knowledge that he made far fewer mistakes than he had the first day.

The next morning, he moved in. As the moving men

were bringing his furniture into the apartment, he had two callers. The first was a stout, gray-haired Negro lady, who introduced herself and said that Mr. Resnikoff (who could be no one else but the Resident Manager) had told her that he might be needing someone to clean for him. She was the housekeeper for 10-C, and her employer, an elderly widow, had no objection to her making a little extra money. For thirty dollars a week, it was agreed that she would clean the apartment, make the bed, and see that his laundry was sent out and delivered. She added, as she left, that the way the building switchboard was set up, she could, if he wanted, take telephone messages for him when he was out during the day.

The second caller was the installer from the telephone company. He put in a private telephone and left. Tony made two calls, first to his home, where his grandfather answered and was glad to hear that he was with "his own people." He was so pleased, in fact, that Tony was spared the standard speech that his place was home with the family, not running around alone in the big city. Then his father came on the phone, and Tony gave him his new telephone number and address.

"Where?" his father asked. Tony repeated the address. "How much are they paying you? More important how much are you paying?"

"Two hundred."

"And what else do you have to do? Take out the garbage? Polish the floors?"

"As a matter of fact, Dad, I am waiting on tables."

"I don't think I want to hear the rest of this," his father

said. "When you come to your senses, and want an honest job, you can come home."

Then Tony called Collier, Richards & Company. They knew where he had been staying at the hotel, and they just might want to get in touch with him. He asked for Miss Chedister, and she was out, so he got the blonde receptionist instead and gave her the new address, and the new phone number, and the message that unless he heard from the company to the contrary, he would be in for work on Monday morning.

And then he rushed over to the Golden Samovar in time for the luncheon business.

4

On Sunday afternoon, while he was sitting with his feet up on the window sill, content just to watch Central Park out in front of him, the door buzzer sounded, and he opened it to find Mr. Orlovsky, Leo, and Leo's mother. They brought him, and he was deeply touched, an old Russian ikon, a religious object, as a housewarming gift.

He had been able, over the balance of the week, to make Leo understand that he simply wouldn't have the energy to put in a full day at Collier, Richards & Company and then work at night in the Golden Samovar, even if it meant anywhere from thirty-five to sixty dollars a night. He was glad that he had, because he liked Leo, and wanted to keep alive the friendship that had developed between them.

Uncle Pieter and Mrs. Orlovsky left after a while, and Tony and Leo went downtown to a restaurant and bar on Third Avenue which, according to Leo, had a well-deserved reputation for unattached young ladies. The reputation was undeserved, and after spending a couple of

44

hours looking at other young men who apparently had been similarly misinformed, they called it a night.

Leo vowed solemnly that if Tony came for dinner at the Samovar, he would be treated like any other paying customer and not shepherded into a uniform.

At five minutes to nine the next morning, Anthony Fletcher got off the elevator on the 22nd floor of 390 Park Avenue and was greeted by name by the receptionist.

"Good morning, Mr. Fletcher," she said. "Your office is waiting for you. Let me show you where it is."

She led him down a corridor to a pastel blue door on which was written in gold: MR. FLETCHER. She pushed it open, and Tony looked in on a small office. He had just decided that it was maybe two square feet larger than his last office had been when a young woman came into it from another office.

"You must be Mr. Fletcher," she said. "I've been fixing up your desk. I'm Marilyn Dubinsky, your new secretary —or I will be, if that's all right with you."

"How do you do?" Tony said.

"It's right in there," she said, indicating his office. "You can almost see Park Avenue."

"Gee whiz," Tony said, and almost immediately regretted his sarcasm. He went into his new office. He had a desk, and a high-backed chair, a coffee table, a couch, a telephone table behind the desk, and a two-pen pen holder. There was a telephone and a water carafe and a calendar. There was a typewriter, a dictating machine and an intercom. He had all the equipment he would need to go to work, everything but some work to do.

Collier, Richards & Company had started something new in his absence. It was a mimeographed legal length sheet of paper called the ColRiCO NEWS. It looked very much like a standard Army Daily Bulletin, and he half expected to find his name somewhere in it as Officer of The Day or Officer of the Guard. He did find his name, in item 17:

17. OFFICE ASSIGNMENT:
    AMEND INTEROFFICE AND
    NATIONAL PHONE BOOKS
    AS FOLLOWS:
    Add:
    FLETCHER, Mr. Anthony, 22–102.
                    Extension 201 Research
                    & Creativity Committee
        Secretary: Miss DUBINSKY,
                    Marilyn 22–101 Extension 202

At eleven o'clock, just after Mr. Anthony Fletcher had carefully calculated that there were 528 windows in the building across from his, and that there were 288 foot-square acoustin tiles in the ceiling of his 12 x 24-foot office, the telephone buzzed discreetly. He grabbed it, picked it up, and got a dial tone. The telephone continued to ring, or buzz. Somewhat belatedly remembering that you had to push the flashing button, he pushed it.

"Did I interrupt anything, Tony?" Skeezix James asked.

"Not a thing," Tony said.

"When you can find the time, Tony, I wish you'd check

46

with the film library, and eyeball the kinescopes of Brisk and Dulcet."

"Be glad to. Anything particular I should be looking for?" Brisk was a deodorant; Dulcet a hair tonic.

"Just eyeball them, and give them a think," Skeezix said. "No hurry. And I'll get back to you."

The phone clicked. Skeezix habitually omitted expressions of greeting and farewell. They were unduly time consuming, in his opinion. He was probably right, but it was still a little unnerving.

Tony examined the push buttons of his intercom. There were a number of buttons, but none of them read "Film Library." None of them, either, he realized, said "Mr. James." He was apparently not high enough in the hierarchy to have direct access to James. There was a button marked "Secty." He pushed it.

"Yes, Mr. Fletcher?"

"I'd like to look at the kinescopes of Brisk and Dulcet," he said. "How would I go about doing that?"

"Well," she said. "You could call the film library. Their extension is 505. Didn't I leave you a phone book?"

"Yes, you did," Tony said. "Pardon me."

He called the film library.

"This is Tony Fletcher," he said. "How much trouble would it be for me to look at the kinescopes of Dulcet and Brisk?"

"Which ones did you have in mind, Mr. Fletcher?"

"All of them, I suppose," Tony said.

"They go back ten years," the voice said. "That's a lot of film."

47

"When would it be convenient for me to screen them?" Tony countered.

"Have you got a screen in your office?" the film librarian asked.

"Wait a minute," Tony said. He pushed the Secty. button again.

"Yes, Mr. Fletcher?"

"Have I got a projection screen in here?"

"No, Mr. Fletcher," she said, and then, very sweetly, "I guess you could use the wall. It's flat and white."

"Thank you very much, Miss Dubinsky," he said, and then: "I'll show them on the wall. Can I borrow a projector?"

"I'll send a projectionist with the film, Mr. Fletcher, just the minute he's free."

"Thanks very much," Tony said. He opened a drawer, took out a fresh legal pad, and a fresh pencil and wrote on it: "IMPRESSIONS OF BRISK AND DULCET KINESCOPES."

Then he settled down to wait for the projectionist, the projector, and the film.

He waited just over an hour, and then called the film library again. A new voice told him that the projectionist must have gone to lunch, but that he would be dispatched just as soon as he was available.

Miss Dubinsky's voice came over the intercom. "Would it be all right if I went to lunch now, Mr. Fletcher? Or is there something you'd like me to do?"

"Go ahead, Miss Dubinsky," he said. That meant, of course, that he would have to wait until she returned.

Otherwise, the projectionist would be likely to show up, find his office deserted, and leave.

Miss Dubinsky apparently took long lunch hours. It was twenty-five after one before she returned. The projectionist hadn't shown up. He gave the matter of the hour and twenty-five-minute lunch hour some thought and stopped by Miss Dubinsky's desk on his way out.

"I wish, in the future, Miss Dubinsky, that if you're going to need more than an hour for lunch, you'd let me know beforehand."

"Very well," she said, obviously indignant; Tony was going to be *that* kind of a boss.

He had a roast beef sandwich and a glass of milk in the building drugstore cafeteria and was back in his office in less than forty minutes. A projector had been set up, and there was a stack of film cans two feet high beside it.

He pushed Miss Dubinsky's button. "Where did the projectionist go?" he asked.

"He got here right after you left. I told him you had strong feelings about a 60-minute lunch hour, and he said he'd be back at half-past two."

"Thank you," he said. He had the choice between waiting the twenty minutes, calling the film library again to find the projectionist, or, the obvious answer, running the projector himself.

He drew the blinds in the office, threaded the film, adjusted the legal pad, turned the lights off, and ran the film.

By the time the first 60-second commercial was over, Tony knew that he was going to have to come pretty

49

close to hypocrisy, or else get himself in trouble, when discussing his impression of the commercials. He had what he realized was an out-of-step opinion of deodorants; his solution to the problem of an unpleasant smelling body was a liberal application of soap and water, taken as often as necessary. He did not, in other words, use a deodorant. Neither did he use hair tonic. He had healthy hair, closely cropped, and all he needed was a comb and a brush.

He was aware, however, that the deodorant and hair tonic industry was a multimillion-dollar business, and that the manufacturers of Brisk and Dulcet were major clients of Collier, Richards & Company. The Brisk/Dulcet/Tart (a mouthwash) account executive was a major executive within the firm, a vice-president and a pillar of the company.

Tony decided that he would limit his comments to professional ones, comparing these kinescopes with the competition's commercials, and perhaps offering a word of comment here and there about the actors and actresses in the commercials, the language, and so on.

There was more than half an hour of film on each spool. Before it had run out, however, his door was opened, light flooded the room, and a tall young man came in.

"Hey, what's going on?" he demanded.

"Who are you?"

"I'm from the film library. I'm supposed to show kinescopes to Mr. Fletcher. Who're you?"

"Where were you when I needed you?" Tony said. "I'm Fletcher. Didn't your mother teach you to knock?"

"There's nobody out there," the young man said. "Sorry. You know," he said, and now there was just a suggestion of underling-to-superior tone in his voice, "I'm supposed to run the projector, Mr. Fletcher."

Tony lost his temper. "So far as I'm concerned, you can take the rest of the afternoon off. Everybody else seems to have taken off, anyway, and I'm perfectly able to run the projector myself."

"It's not procedure," the young man said.

"Tell your boss to write me a memorandum," Tony said. "Thank you, and good-bye."

"Have it your way," the young man said, and left, closing the door behind him.

Tony restarted the projector, finished that spool of film, rewound it, put a new one on, and spent the rest of the afternoon watching film. He became aware that it was getting close to quitting time. At ten minutes to five, the intercom spoke:

"Is it all right if I go, Mr. Fletcher?" Miss Dubinsky asked.

"Where have you been, Miss Dubinsky?" he asked.

"Well, there didn't seem to be much doing around here, so I went back where I used to work and talked to the girls."

"The next time you do that, will you ask permission, first?"

"Yes, sir," she said. "And would you like me to stick

51

around until precisely five o'clock, *Mister* Fletcher?"

"No, you can run along, Miss Dubinsky," he said.

He refused to let himself get angry. He was embarrassed that he'd jumped all over the projectionist. He'd been wrong about that. This wasn't the orderly room, nor the army, and running the projector had been his job. But he was afraid that the business with Miss Dubinsky was not yet over.

By the time he'd run all the cans of film, it was almost seven o'clock. He rewound the last reel and looked at the sheet of legal paper on which he'd written: IMPRESSIONS OF BRISK AND DULCET KINESCOPES.

Tony Fletcher was an accomplished visual artist; he'd begun that way in the advertising business when that surprising talent had been uncovered in college. It came out now. There were a series of doodles on the yellow, lined page. They were all quite good faces, and each face rather skillfully showed human beings, male, female, young and old, registering utter disgust on their faces.

Tony quickly tore off the page, balled it up, and threw it into his wastebasket. It was not, and he knew it, the proper attitude to have.

He shut off the lights in his office and left the building. He started to walk over to Fifth Avenue, realized he was hungry, went into a restaurant and ate dinner without, once the food was before him, much of an appetite. Then he went home and watched television, paying particular attention to the hair tonic and deodorant commercials of the competition. They had a great deal in common, he thought, with the Brisk and Dulcet commercials. They were just as much an affront to good taste.

Miss Dubinsky, surprisingly, was on duty in his office when he got there in the morning. She smiled at him, said "Good morning," and handed him the little yellow form on which telephone calls were recorded.

He returned her good morning and took the little yellow form with him into his office. He was pleased with what it said: "Miss Chedister of the personnel department called and would like to see you at your earliest convenience."

He got out the book, found her number, and dialed it.

"Miss Chedister," she said, very properly.

"Good morning, Miss Chedister," he said. "This is Tony Fletcher."

"Thank you for calling so quickly, Mr. Fletcher," she said. "I wonder when you could fit me into your schedule?"

"Right now, if that's all right with you," Tony said. "Should I come down there?"

"Oh, no. I'll be right up."

Tony had time, before she got there, to examine himself in the mirror above the basin in the combined washroom-clothes closet off his office. He thought he looked very decent, an up-and-coming young advertising type.

"Miss Chedister to see you, Mr. Fletcher," Miss Dubinsky's voice announced from the intercom.

Feeling somewhat like the Chairman of the Board, Tony replied, "Would you ask her to come right in, please?"

53

Miss Dubinsky, smiling broadly, held the door open for Miss Chedister.

"Good morning," Tony said. "Won't you sit down? What can I do for you?"

Miss Chedister waited until Miss Dubinsky had closed the door behind her.

"I don't quite know how to start," she said.

"Try the beginning," he said. She looked great, he thought. A rare combination of good looks and brains. Plus she was a blonde. Opposites, he thought, aware that he was dark, attract.

"Your secretary has asked to be relieved of her assignment," she said. "She was waiting for me in the personnel office when I got there this morning."

"Oh," Tony said. For some reason he was embarrassed. "So now what happens?"

"I thought perhaps I could smooth things over between you. After all, she just started to work for you."

"So far," Tony said, "she's sharpened a couple of pencils and told me, in effect, to look up my own numbers in the phone book. Did that wear her out?"

"You needn't be sarcastic," she said.

"We did have a few words," Tony said, and he realized he was angry again. "I let her know that I thought an hour and twenty-five minutes for lunch was twenty-five minutes too long; that I didn't appreciate her taking off in the middle of the afternoon to chat with the ladies in her previous sector of employment; and she may have detected just the suggestion of annoyance in my voice when I gave her permission to leave ten minutes before quit-

54

ting time. I suppose that qualifies me for the Simon Legree award?"

"There is obviously a personality conflict here," Miss Chedister said.

"Is that what you call it?" Tony asked.

"Don't use that tone of voice to me, please, Mr. Fletcher," Miss Chedister said.

"I beg your pardon," Tony said.

"I think the best thing to do under the circumstances is try to arrange a replacement for Miss Dubinsky for you," Miss Chedister said. "I think that would be the best thing, to start over with a fresh page on both sides."

"You've already decided I'm a bad guy," Tony said. "So let's make it official. I don't like her running to complain to you first thing in the morning; I don't think she'll prove to be a satisfactory secretary. I want a replacement, and I want one who understands the eight-hour day, the 60-minute lunch hour, and the quitting time of five o'clock. OK?"

"It may take some time to recruit a replacement," Miss Chedister said.

"Since I have very little to do anyway, I don't consider that an insurmountable problem," Tony said. "Why don't you just take her with you on your way out?"

"You're going to have to learn, Mr. Fletcher," Miss Chedister said, red-faced, "that you're out of the army, and that you just can't order people around here as you apparently did in the army."

"When you're recruiting a replacement," Tony said, sarcastic and angry, "see if you can't find me a comfortable middle-aged woman. I have this personality defect, you see, I can't stand bright young females."

Icily, she said: "Thank you for giving me so much of your valuable time, Mr. Fletcher."

"Simple military courtesy, Miss Chedister," he said. She slammed the door on her way out.

He waited fifteen minutes and then went into his outer office. The desk occupied by Miss Dubinsky had been cleaned off. The typewriter was covered, and it was as if she had never been there.

This, Tony thought, was what was called getting off to a flying start.

He spent the rest of the morning forcing himself to think about the kinescopes he'd watched the day before, trying very hard, and succeeding not at all, to offer constructive criticism. Just about the time he thought he'd go out for lunch, the phone rang. It was James again:

"I don't suppose you've had time to check with the film library?" he asked, without a previous word of greeting.

"I ran all they had yesterday," Tony said.

"Good boy. I hope you're free for lunch. You're not romancing that new secretary of yours, are you?"

"No, sir," Tony said. "You have my oath as a gentleman."

"Have lunch with me then, Tony, there's some people I want you to meet. More accurately, there are some people who I want to meet you."

"Can I ask who? *Whom?*"

"Vice-President, Merchandising, and Director, Advertising, for Conshohocken Consolidated Chemical."

"Oh," Tony said. On every package of Brisk, Dul-cet and Tart was a small logotype, made up of three C's. Two were back to back, and the third rested upside down on top of them. It stood for Conshohocken Consolidated Chemical.

"We are going to meet them at Luchow's," James said. "Vice-President, Merchandising, is big on German chow. Pick me up here at five to one?"

"Yes, sir," Tony said.

"Five to one," James repeated, and then hung up without a good-bye.

5

Vice President, Merchandising, whose title, in Skeezix James's somewhat impolite but inarguably effective manner of getting to the important things first, was more important than his name, was waiting for them on the sidewalk outside Luchow's Restaurant when they got out of the taxi.

He was a tall, bony man, whose expensive clothing hung loosely on him, and when he smiled and put out his hand, he displayed a great many large and healthy teeth.

"Hello, Skeezix," he said. "Good to see you."

"Nice to see you, Tom," Skeezix said. "I'd like you to meet Tony Fletcher. Tony, this is Mr. Cantarella, of CCC."

"How do you do, sir?" Tony said. Cantarella's handshake was firm.

"I'm glad to meet you," he said. "I saw the story in *The Times.*"

"I had nothing to do with that story," Tony said. "That was the boss's idea."

"Never hide your light under a bushel," Cantarella said.

"Where's Gibbons?" Skeezix asked.

"He got hung up downtown, I suppose. Let's go inside. He'll be along."

There was a buffet. Tony was very fond of buffets and took full advantage of this one, despite a disquieting feeling in his stomach that there was going to be more to this luncheon than a good meal and some pleasant conversation. He decided that he would follow the old army maxim of keeping his ears open and his mouth shut.

He soon found out that this was exactly the opposite of what Skeezix and Mr. Cantarella had in mind; that he was, in fact, the reason they were having lunch.

It began, in fact, as soon as they had taken a table, and a waiter had brought them glasses of dark beer. Skeezix, skillfully and tactfully, but nonetheless embarrassing to Tony, began with a recitation of Tony's past achievements, starting in college (where Tony had drawn the sketch of the rough-looking truck driver carrying the egg on a pillow, which decorated all Fletcher Trucking Company rolling stock) and his pre-service work for Collier, Richards & Company, Corey Rubber and Blackman Boats.

Cantarella was familiar with those advertising campaigns, which were slightly offbeat, if not quite mod or psychedelic or whatever word was now used to describe the far-out. He asked Tony about his service, and volun-

59

teered the information that he had kept his reserve commission active and recommended that Tony consider doing the same thing.

Tony was sensitive enough to realize that he was being judged by Cantarella, and that he was apparently passing the test.

"Skeezix tells me he's going to have you take a look at our campaigns over the past couple of years," Cantarella said.

"I had a look at the kinescopes of the television commercials," Tony said. "I haven't had a chance to examine the other media."

"Well, Tony, what's your opinion?" Cantarella said. "You haven't been inspired to rush right out to the drugstore for a can of Brisk?" His voice was joking, but Tony knew his answer would be weighed.

"I'm just getting re-accustomed to inside plumbing," he said.

Cantarella laughed, and then said, looking up: "Oh, here's Gibbons." Because Skeezix looked, Tony decided it would be all right if he looked, too. He turned and found himself looking at the young man who'd brought Barbara Chedister to the Golden Samovar, the one he'd tricked into the horseradish sandwich, the one who had tipped waiter Boris a lousy ten per cent. He looked just as surprised as Tony did.

"You know Skeezix, of course," Cantarella said. "And this is Anthony Fletcher. Fletcher, this is Bob Gibbons."

Tony understood, as he stood up to shake Gibbons' hand, that Gibbons was to Cantarella as he was to Skeezix. A subordinate, first, but a subordinate with potential.

"How are you?" Gibbons said. "We've met, haven't we?"

"Oh, have you?" Cantarella asked. "Where?"

"Unless I'm really flipping my cork right here in Luchow's," Gibbons said, "you are—or at least, *were*, a waiter in a Russian restaurant."

"That's right," Tony said. "The Golden Samovar."

"Really?" Cantarella asked. "What was that, real market research?"

It was fairly standard practice in the advertising business to send copywriters and others charged with developing advertising campaigns to work in stores, to go out in public and listen to what people were saying. The path of least resistance would have been for Tony to imply that had been the case here. But that would have been dishonest, and Tony could think of no reason why he should be ashamed of having done an honest night's work.

"No," he said. "I was working as a waiter in the Golden Samovar."

"Before you went to work for Collier, Richards?" Cantarella asked.

"No. Last week," Tony said.

"Extraordinary."

"Tony's an extraordinary chap," Skeezix said. "I found out last week that he has an apartment on Fifth, across from the Park, complete with maid, just down the block from where the President used to live."

61

"Are you paying him that kind of money?" Cantarella asked.

"No. That's probably why he's moonlighting in a Russian restaurant," James said. "He needs the money."

"It's a long story," Tony said.

"We have all the time in the world," Cantarella said. "And it sounds fascinating."

"The guy who owns the restaurant is a friend of mine," Tony said. "Another Russian. He was short a waiter, and I volunteered. I made about three hundred bucks, by the way. And the same guy arranged the apartment for me. It's what used to be the chauffeur's quarters."

"And the maid?"

"How did you hear about that?"

"Oh, when you called in your new phone, I immediately called back. 'Mr. Fletcher's residence,' the lady said, and when I asked who she might be, she said she was 'one of the maids.' At that point, I decided that I'd just wait until you came to work and then I would give you the penny saved, penny earned speech."

"I'm paying less for the new apartment than I paid for the last one I had, and, as you recall, the last one was hardly luxurious."

"I'm awed to find that someone has actually beat the high rent business," Cantarella said, and from his tone, Tony sensed that he had not embarrassed the company by what he'd done. He also sensed that Gibbons would have liked it the other way around; he hadn't tactfully skirted the subject, but had jumped right in.

"You got here just in time, Bob," Cantarella said. "We

had just asked Tony what he thought of the last couple of campaigns."

"And what did Tony say?" Gibbons asked.

"Tony said," Tony said with a smile, "that Tony didn't think he was qualified to offer an opinion."

"Can I read that to mean you don't like the campaigns, but are reluctant to say that in front of the boss and the company's advertising director?" Gibbons asked.

"That's a little rough, Bob," Cantarella protested.

"We're all friends," Gibbons said. "Aren't we?"

"Let's hear it, Tony," Skeezix said, and Tony was aware that he was floundering, that he didn't know whether he was expected to say nice things.

"To tell you the truth, they don't appeal to me," he said.

"In what way?" Cantarella asked, still smiling.

"I think they're too cute," Tony said. "They embarrass me."

He realized, immediately, that had been the wrong thing to say. Skeezix was still smiling, but he looked as if he had suddenly been painfully pinched. Mr. Cantarella looked thoughtful; Gibbons looked, behind a look of shock, delighted.

What have I done to him, Tony asked himself, and then answered with the bread and horseradish and vodka. But he knew it was more than that. For some reason, he had what Barbara had called a "personality conflict" with this guy.

"You asked for it, Skeezix," Cantarella said. "And you got it."

63

"How do they embarrass you, Fletcher?" Gibbons asked.

"I don't know," Tony said, somewhat lamely. "They just do. Maybe because I'm in the business." He paused, and then repeated, "I don't know. They embarrass me."

The others looked at him. He knew he had to say something.

"In a professional sense, they're well done. I watched the competition last night, and ours are better. That's not just loyalty, either."

"If anything, Fletcher," Cantarella said, "I believe that you do speak your mind."

"I've obviously said the wrong thing," Tony said. "I don't know whether or not I should apologize. But you ought to be grateful that I'm not doing your copy."

"But you will be," Cantarella said, slowly and deliberately.

"I beg your pardon?" Tony asked.

"As a matter of fact, Fletcher," Cantarella said, "personally, our commercials offend me, too. I have a son, several years younger than you are, who winces whenever they come on television. That bothers me two ways. I don't like being responsible for something that embarrasses me and pains my son. And it has occurred to me that we just might be chasing other customers away with our commercials. Tell me, do you use Brisk yourself?"

"No, sir."

"Neither does my son," Cantarella said. "And I think a good market analysis would indicate that you and he aren't alone."

"I don't think I could do any better than what's being done," Tony said.

"Neither do I," Cantarella said. "But we want to try it anyway. We're not going to make any major changes in our present scheduled campaign. But, presuming you can come up with something, we'll try a test market somewhere."

"I've never done anything like this," Tony said, desperately wanting to get out of this assignment. "My whole experience has been with tires and boats."

"Advertising designed to appeal to men," Skeezix said, very effectively cutting his throat. "And that, sport, is how we sell deodorant."

"I don't know, Skeezix," Tony said.

"Yours not to reason why, yours but to put your talent where your mouth was," Skeezix said. "You're fresh—by that I mean, brand-new—Tony. You're good. That's why we're paying you all that money. I know a lot of people who would welcome the chance to try to improve the class of commercials."

"I'm not the deodorant type, I guess," Tony said.

"That's a good place to start," Cantarella said. "Start by finding out what would make you buy a large economy size of Brisk."

"OK," Tony said. "I'll do my best."

"How do you plan to start?" Gibbons asked. It was not a simple question, or one even of idle curiosity. Tony sensed that Gibbons was making a play to be considered one of the three big shots dealing with the flunky. He didn't think Gibbons had that right.

65

"Unless Mr. Cantarella or Mr. James have any suggestions," Tony said, with a bright smile, "I think I'll start with digging. Unless you've got some ideas?"

"No," Gibbons said. "But I'd like to see what you come up with."

"I certainly have no objection to you seeing it," Tony said. "If Mr. Cantarella doesn't mind."

Gibbons flushed. Cantarella laughed. "Sharpen your scalpel, Bob," he said. "When Skeezix and I have shot holes in Tony's bright new balloons, we'll give you a chance."

"I thought I'd be working with Tony on this," Gibbons said smoothly.

"I think it would be better if we gave Tony his head," Cantarella said. "You sort of represent the establishment, Bob. You might influence him."

"I'd like to be kept up to date on what he's doing," Gibbons went on doggedly.

"You will be," Cantarella said, and his tone of voice closed the subject.

In the taxi on the way back to the office, Tony tried, and failed, to get Skeezix to let him off the hook.

"This is not my bright idea, Tony," he said. "Tom Cantarella saw that story in *The Times*—including, I must admit, that line about the Research and Creativity— He called me up and proposed this. I couldn't tell him no. He came right to me, not even through the account executive."

"I imagine this is going to make me very popular with him, too," Tony said.

66

"I'll keep him off your back," Skeezix said. "You just come up with something that is better. Or even—I'll be satisfied if what you come up with is nearly as good as what's being done."

It was half-past three before they got back to the office. By the time Tony had requested, and the film library had delivered, the kinescopes of the competitive advertising campaign, it was quarter after four.

The same projectionist delivered the film and the projector. This time he knocked.

"Still no secretary," he said.

"She requested relief," Tony told him. "I gathered she didn't like me."

"I've crossed words with that girl before," the projectionist said. "You're probably better off without her."

"I think I like you," Tony said. "What did you say your name was?"

"Lewis," the projectionist said. "Bill Lewis."

"How long have you been projecting for the company?"

"Couple of weeks. I'm a trainee. I worked in the mailroom. I was a messenger. I clipped newspaper ads in market analysis. And now I'm a projectionist. The theory is that I'll learn something while watching the film unwind."

"It's not a bad theory," Tony said. "Welcome to the club." Then he had an idea. "Do they pay you overtime?"

"Time and a half."

"You can make some tonight, if you want to," he said. "I'm about to soak myself in deodorant commercials."

"I can use the money," Lewis said. "Could I use your phone to call my wife?"

"Be my guest," Tony said. "I'm sorry I jumped on you yesterday."

"Forget it," Lewis said. "Around here, I'm used to it."

The projector ran until half past nine, as Tony methodically broke down the competition's advertising into categories. Humor. Practicality. Human Insecurity. Romance. Status.

He sent out for sandwiches and a pot of coffee about seven-thirty, and made a note to turn in an expense voucher for them. If you worked at night, the company fed you.

By nine-thirty, his head hurt, and he'd had enough.

"If you can put up with it," he said. "We'll do it again in the morning. You want to stop and get a beer someplace?"

"Let me take a raincheck, Mr. Fletcher," Lewis said. "My wife'll be expecting me."

"Call me Tony," Tony said.

"OK," Lewis said, and he put out his hand. "I appreciate you letting me in on this."

"Misery loves company," Tony said. "See you in the morning."

When he walked out of the building, Tony decided that he wanted that beer. He didn't really know where to go, and a taxi came by, so he flagged it and gave the driver the address of the Golden Samovar.

He went in and squeezed up to the bar and got immediate service. He'd taken a couple of sips of the beer when one of the waiters touched his sleeve and told him

Leo wanted to see him in the kitchen. Carrying the beer glass, he walked through the restaurant and into the kitchen and over to Leo, who was slicing a round of beef.

"Your lady friend was in, Romeo," he said. "She was very disturbed you weren't here."

"What lady friend?"

"*What* lady friend? Come *on*, Lover. The good-looking blonde with the red glasses. She said she'd tried your apartment, so *she* must know you. Out with somebody else, were you?"

"I was working," Tony said. There was no question about it, Barbara Chedister had been looking for him. "Can I use your phone?"

"You don't mean to tell me you remember who she is?"

"Try not to slice your thumb off," Tony said, and went into the office and took out the Manhattan telephone directory. There it was CHEDISTER, Brbra, 145 E 83rd.

He dialed the number.

"Yes?" She sounded tired and discouraged.

"Tony Fletcher, Miss Chedister," he said. "I understand you were looking for me."

"You got my message?" she asked.

"No. I just came in the Samovar for a beer, and Leo told me you'd been in."

"I called your apartment," she said, and then she stopped, and there was a long pause.

"Checking up on my off-duty hours, are you?" Tony asked, "or was there something else on your mind?"

"Don't come on so strong," she said. "I was about to apologize."

"For what?"

69

"For the crack I made in your office," she said. "That wasn't fair. And there's something else, too."

"What?"

"I can't ask you up here," she said. "My landlady's got a thing about gentlemen callers after ten. Could you meet me someplace?"

"Name it," Tony said.

"There's a Jewish delicatessen on the corner of 80th and Third Avenue," she said. "Could you meet me there?"

"I'll be waiting for you," he said. He hung up and paused long enough by Leo's shoulder to tell him he hoped that he and the round of beef would be very happy, and then walked over to the delicatessen.

He was wrong. She'd beat him there. She was still wearing the red-rimmed glasses, but the fancy makeup was gone, and she was wearing a sweater and a skirt and looked, in Tony's opinion, much better than she did when wearing her executive clothes.

"Hi," he said.

"The trouble with these places is that they always make me hungry," she said.

"So let's get something to eat," Tony said. "All I had for dinner was an egg salad sandwich."

"Dutch," she said. "I didn't call you up to mooch a meal."

"I'm the last of the big spenders," he said. "Providing you don't order more than a dollar and a quarter's worth."

They both ordered roast beef on rye and coffee. She didn't seem overly anxious to say what she had come to

70

say, so he let her wait until she had finished her sandwich.

"Let me start at the beginning," she said. "After we had our pleasant little chat in the office this morning, I began to have the radical idea that maybe there were two sides to that story, too. So I did a little checking on Miss Dubinsky. The reason, I found out, that Scheduling was so anxious to provide a highly recommended secretary to Mr. Fletcher was less altruistic interest in the efficiency of the firm, than in that of the Scheduling Department. I found out that she has a reputation for coming in late—when she does come in—and for taking off early, and for taking extended lunch periods. When she's in the office, she has the well-earned reputation of being the best conversationalist around."

"Oh," Tony said.

"So, it occurred to me that I owed you an apology."

"Forget it."

"I've hardly begun," she said. "When I got on the subject of apologies, it occurred to me that I had no right to make that crack about you having to learn you were out of the army."

"Forget that, too," Tony said. "You and I had what is called a 'personality conflict.'"

She laughed and smiled at him, and he thought she smiled very well.

"OK. So I made up my mind that I would (a) get you a secretary a good bit sooner than I had planned to get you one and (b) stop by your office in the morning and apologize."

"This is much nicer," Tony said. "I'm always carried

away by the romance of a good Jewish delicatessen."

"I'm still not finished," she said. "I had a gentleman caller early this evening. I was surprised, because we really hadn't hit it off on the couple of times I'd gone out with him. You've met him. Twice. Once when you made him eat that horseradish to prove what a big, strong man he was, and today, over lunch."

"Gibbons," Tony said. "Why do you go out with him, if you don't like him?"

"The rumors that I have gentlemen admirers lined up in a column of twos is unfortunately not true. Besides, he always takes me to expensive restaurants. He insists on it, and he can afford it."

"What did he want?"

"He couldn't say enough nice things about you," Barbara said. "He thought it was a splendid joke, etcetera etcetera. He's pretty transparent. What he wanted was information about you. Where you went to school, how much money you're making, and so on."

"Why?"

"I gathered that you had some sort of a run-in at lunch, and he came out losers."

Tony told her what had happened.

"Well, I thought it would be something like that," she said. "Anyway, he's obviously got it in for you, and he's in a position to do you a lot of harm, and it just seemed fair that I tell you about it."

"He doesn't worry me," Tony said, thinking out loud. "His boss, and for that matter, my boss, worry me."

"Why?" Barbara asked. "What did you say to them?"

"They expect something from me that I don't think I can produce," he said.

"The Boy Wonder's turning modest?"

"The Boy Wonder is really a very practical guy, under all the glitter and shine," he said. "And somewhat out of tune with the rest of the orchestra. I just can't work up a bona fide enthusiasm for deodorant, mouthwash and hair tonic."

"What will you do, Tony?" she asked. "I mean, if you really can't—"

"I can always go back to driving a truck," he said. "Maybe that's what I really should be doing anyway."

She looked at him, and he thought he saw genuine sympathy, not pity, but sympathetic interest in her eyes. He thought that if he went back to Fletcher Trucking, he would be a long way from Manhattan and Miss Barbara Chedister.

"You mean, quit?" she asked.

"First," he said aloud as he thought it, "I'm going to give it the Old School Try."

"Good for you," she said, and apparently without thinking about it, she reached out and touched his hand. His face showed his surprise, and when she saw that she quickly withdrew her hand and flushed.

"Don't get the wrong idea," he said. "I sort of liked that."

"This is supposed to be a business conference," she said.

"It didn't turn out that way, did it?" Tony replied. "It's more like the signing of an armistice and a mutual assistance treaty. Although I don't really know what I could do for you."

"You could walk me home," she said.

She took his arm as they walked to her apartment, and he thought that was just fine.

6

At eleven o'clock the next morning, Miss Chedister of the Personnel Department went to the office of Anthony Fletcher, followed by a gray-haired woman who appeared to be in her late forties.

There was no secretary in the outer office, of course, so they knocked at the inner door and were told to enter. They found Mr. Fletcher with his feet up on the desk, watching commercials for competitive deodorants being projected on the wall.

"Am I interrupting anything, Mr. Fletcher?" Miss Chedister asked.

"Yes, you are, and I'm very grateful," Mr. Fletcher said. "Another ninety seconds of that and I would be out of my skull. Rewind it, Bill, will you?"

He snapped the office lights on, and only then saw the older woman with Barbara. He quickly got to his feet.

"Mr. Fletcher, this is Mrs. Berkowitz."

"How do you do?" Tony said.

75

"Mrs. Berkowitz is an old hand at Collier, Richards," Barbara said, "who's been away for a while."

"Oh?"

"Twenty years, Mr. Fletcher," the older woman said. "I raised a family."

"I see," Tony said, not quite sure what to make of the whole business.

"And now, skills a little rusty," she said, "I'm back, looking for a job."

"I thought you two might get along," Barbara said.

"Oh," Tony said, now understanding. "Well, come on in, Mrs. Berkowitz, and drag up a pencil."

"Just like that?" she asked. "I told you I'm awful rusty on shorthand."

"But you can type?"

"I can still type," she said.

"Well, you can't be nearly as rusty as I am inept," Tony said. "Did Miss Chedister tell you what we're trying to do in here?"

"More or less," she said.

"If you can put up with me," Tony said, "and acres and acres of deodorant cans, we'd love to have you."

"That was quick," she said. "I accept."

"I trust Miss Chedister's judgment," Tony said.

"Why, thank you, Mr. Fletcher," Barbara said.

"Can I express my appreciation by buying you lunch, Miss Chedister?" Tony went on.

She paused, and then said: "I think you'll be too busy for that, Mr. Fletcher. But if you're going to quit at a reasonable hour tonight, maybe we could have a sandwich."

76

"Eight o'clock?" Tony asked. "Your place, or that lovely delicatessen?"

"I'll wait for you in the deli," Barbara said, and left.

"She's a nice girl," Mrs. Berkowitz said, when the door closed behind her.

"Mrs. Berkowitz, you are obviously a woman of sound judgment," Tony said.

"With three sons and no daughters, you get to be a good judge of other people's daughters," she said. "Is there anything you'd like me to do?"

"You might as well watch the movies," Tony said. "Then you'll know as much as Bill and I do. This is Bill Lewis, by the way, our long-suffering projectionist."

They shook hands, Bill Lewis pulled up a chair for Mrs. Berkowitz, the lights were put out, and the projector started to roll again.

Mrs. Berkowitz, at half-past twelve, when Tony's growling stomach announced that it was time to eat, almost immediately proved her worth. Tony asked her to send out for a "couple of sandwiches and a pot of coffee."

She wasn't gone long, but when she returned, she carried a large paper bag whose delightful aroma preceded her. She'd come up with a lunch, rather than a couple of sandwiches. Hot roast beef, potato salad, a sliced tomato, milk, and tea and coffee.

"I had to leave a deposit for the plates and the cups and saucers," she said, "but I just don't like sandwiches and coffee in a paper container."

About quitting time, Tony began to have the first seed of an idea. He asked Mrs. Berkowitz to arrange to get for him a drawing board, some paper, charcoal, the materials

77

he would need to rough out a story board. When he asked her, he thought that she would probably be able to get the stuff by noon of the next day, which would give him that night and the next morning to do some more thinking.

At quarter after five she was back, pushing a drawing board ahead of her with one hand, and holding a large paper bag full of artist's supplies in the other.

"It's not exactly according to procedure," she said, when he relieved her of the bag. "But I knew Harry Rielly when I was here before." Mr. Rielly was Chief, Visual Presentations Division—head artist—of Collier, Richards & Company. "I borrowed this, and told him I'd repay it when our requisition comes through."

"You're marvelous," Tony said.

"There was a telephone call from the employee relations manager. He wanted to put you on the committee for the company boat ride. I told him your schedule just wouldn't permit it," Mrs. Berkowitz said.

"I'll say it again," Tony said. "You're marvelous."

"I'll see you in the morning, Mr. Fletcher," Mrs. Berkowitz said. "If you're going to work, you're liable to forget your appointment with Miss Chedister. I left word for you to be called at half past seven. So answer the phone when it rings."

"Good night, Mrs. Berkowitz," Tony said.

"Good night, Mr. Fletcher," she said, and she was gone. Tony had a moment to consider the painful idea that he still might be blessed with Miss Dubinsky. Then he arranged the drawing board so that it would get the best

78

light. Doing this was not in keeping with the interior decorator's concept of what his office should look like. The best light required that the drawing board be set up right in the middle of his office, facing the door, and blocking a view of his desk.

He thumbtacked the pad of onionskin paper to the board, opened the boxes of pencils and crayons and charcoal, and told himself that he was getting ready for first thing tomorrow morning. What he would do now would be to go home, take a shower, and put on something besides his advertising uniform. He would be, when he met Barbara, freshly shaved, freshly bathed and looking his best.

He looked at his watch. There would be time for a few, very rough, very preliminary sketches. There was no stool to sit on, so he went to the outer office, rolled Mrs. Berkowitz's typist's chair inside, pulled up so that he could rest his rear end on the back of the back-support, chocked it in place with Webster's Collegiate Dictionary and the N.W. Ayer Annual of United States Periodical Publications. Then he sat down at the board and picked up a piece of charcoal, telling himself again that he had a few minutes time for a couple of preliminary sketches.

The telephone rang.

He went to answer it angrily.

"Mr. Fletcher, it's half past seven, and I was asked to call you then."

"Oh," Tony said. "Thanks very much."

He looked at the drawing board. There was a stack of crumpled paper, discarded ideas, on one side, but there were also three completed drawings carefully placed flat on the floor. The problem was by no means over, but at least he was no longer floundering around, completely in the dark.

He quickly washed his hands, pulled up his necktie, rolled down his shirt-cuffs, put on his jacket and left the office.

"You came here straight from work," she said, when he walked to her table in the delicatessen.

"Uh huh."

"How's it going?"

"Let's not talk about it," he said.

"If I ask you a question, Tony, would you give me an honest answer, rather than a gentleman's answer to a lady, or an answer because you think you should?"

"You've lost me. Let's have the question."

"In 36 minutes, the curtain goes up at the ballet," she said.

"Can we get tickets?" he asked.

She laid two tickets on the table. "You're not just being polite?"

"You ever hear of a Russian who didn't like the ballet? That would be like an Italian who didn't like spaghetti," he said.

She smiled at him, and he knew she believed him and was pleased. It was more a case, really, that Tony didn't actively dislike the ballet, rather than that he was a devoted fan. He liked it tonight because Barbara obviously did, and for the more selfish reason that he didn't feel much like being a brilliant conversationalist, or demonstrating the other characteristics of a young man on a date. She would be happy with the ballet, and he would be happy just being with her.

He looked very thoughtful during the performance, in the half dozen times she looked at his face, but the truth of the matter was that for all it mattered to him, it could have been Adolph Grumpelmayer's Trained Dogs, instead of the Corps de Ballet of the City of New York on the stage. His mind was full of other images, most of them aerosol cans of deodorant.

Barbara began to suspect that his mind was on other things than her when they stopped after the ballet at a Chinese restaurant and he absently-mindedly ordered a hamburger and a coke.

"Tony!" she said, just about as shocked as the waiter. He seemed to wake up, and ordered what one is more or less expected to order in a Chinese restaurant.

And at her door (after having considered and deciding in the affirmative whether or not she would let him kiss her good night) when she made herself available, he kissed her cheek, as if she were a small child or a maiden aunt.

"I'm not your maiden aunt," she said.

That woke him up, too, and he looked at her and then kissed her again.

"From one extreme to another," she said, a moment or so later.

"Yeah," he said. "Wow!"

"Good night, Tony," Barbara said, and went into her apartment.

There was an envelope in the IN box when she came to work next morning. She tore it open to find a Collier, Richards & Company interoffice memorandum.

It was half official and half personal:

(1) I've fixed it with Skeezix James to have Bill Lewis work with me as a copywriter trainee. Would you please change his records accordingly and get someone else to run the projector?

(2) Same time, same place, same coffee-stained table in same delicatessen. I got us tickets to the movies.

Tony

She was annoyed; he was taking entirely too much for granted. She picked up the telephone and dialed his extension.

"Oh, good morning, Miss Chedister," Mrs. Berkowitz said. "No, I'm afraid that you can't talk to him. He asked that he not be disturbed. He and Bill are going great guns in there."

"If the great man," Barbara said angrily, "does deign to come off Mount Olympus, would you ask him to call me, please?"

"Sure," Mrs. Berkowitz said.

Mr. Fletcher did not call Miss Chedister during the day. She waited until quitting time, and then she went to his office. Mrs. Berkowitz was gone, but there was all sorts of activity inside. There was a heavy power cable running through the office and into Tony's. She heard more than two voices.

She went to the door and knocked. There was no reply. She knocked again. There was still no reply. She pushed the door open. They were filming something in there. There were bright lights, and a motion picture camera on a tripod, and what looked like two tool kits full of deodorant on the floor.

People were looking at her.

"Mr. Fletcher," she said, as icily as she could. "Can I have a moment with you?"

He came bounding to the door, tieless, slightly dirty.

"Not now," he said. "I'm busy, Barbara. See you at the deli at quarter to eight."

She opened her mouth to tell him that, for his information, she had other plans for the evening. She didn't get a chance to say a word. He kissed her, right in front of all those people, put his hand on her arm, turned her around, and closed the door.

She did not have the courage to charge back in there and give him a good belt in the face, which was what such behavior deserved. She would settle his hash later, with consummate skill and artistry. Not tonight. What self-respecting person would permit herself to be ordered around like that?

She would no more permit herself to be ordered to appear, like some serf, than she would permit herself to be ordered to jump in the ocean. If Lieutenant Anthony Fletcher, Esquire, thought she would be waiting in the delicatessen as ordered, he had another think coming.

She was there, of course, at quarter to eight, having in

83

the interim convinced herself that telling him off royally, as he certainly deserved, could be far better accomplished in a delicatessen where no one knew either of them, than in the office. She had a couple of things to tell him that would, if she told him in the office, destroy her reputation as a well-bred young lady.

He was five minutes late, and she saw that he had changed clothing. He was wearing a large and contented and pleased smile, which grew even larger when he saw her. She felt her resolve weakening.

"I think the situation is well in hand," he said. "You wouldn't believe how much we got done today."

"Is that so?" she said, half-frozen. "I'm so happy for you."

The sarcasm went right over his head.

"You think it's too early to go lie on the beach?" he asked.

"I beg your pardon?"

"I asked, do you think it's too early, too cold yet, to go lie on the beach?"

"Which beach did you have in mind?" she asked, as sarcastically as she could.

"Belmar, Asbury Park. One of those."

Curiosity got the better of her.

"What in the world are you talking about?"

"I've got to go down there Sunday for a couple of hours, and I thought maybe you'd like to go with me." Then his face fell. "Oh. I suppose your weekend is spoken for, huh? I'm sorry."

She passed up the opportunity to tell him that her

weekend was spoken for. In point of fact, it wasn't, but under the circumstances she felt sure she should have said it was. As well as the days preceding and following the weekend.

"Start from scratch, Tony," she said. "One simple thought at a time."

"OK," he said. "Then you're not busy on Sunday?"

The question took her by surprise and she answered it honestly. "No," she said, and then added hastily, "It happens I'm not. But that doesn't mean I'm going to go to New Jersey with you."

"Why not?" he asked. That kept her off balance.

"I don't know what you plan to do there."

"Well, I've got to go flying for a couple of hours, and what I thought we would do is rent a car, have you drop me off at the airfield, and then pick me up later. You could go lie on the beach, and then we could have dinner, or something. A lobster and some clams."

"You're flying?" she questioned. He nodded. "I thought you were busy with Brisk. So busy that you can't even answer your telephone, or return calls, or have the courtesy to speak to me for a miserable sixty seconds."

"I'm sorry about that," he said. "You got there right at the wrong moment. We were just getting ready to shoot."

"Shoot what?"

"They've got an Auricon in the film library—you know, sound on film?"

"I know what an Auricon camera is," she said.

"Well, I decided I could make a very rough film in just about as much time as I could polish the story boards. So

85

I did. I'm going to show it to James and Cantarella on Monday morning. A whole new slant on the idea."

He was obviously very pleased and happy, and his happiness was contagious. She didn't have the heart to stick a pin in him, and let the good feeling get away.

"Now, what's this about the flying and the beach?"

"Oh, they called up this afternoon, and told me if I hopped right out to Lakewood and got some time over the weekend, I wouldn't have to go through the physical business, or go through anything more than an area checkout. It will be less than 60 days, you see, since I flew the last time."

"In other words," she said, angry and icy again, "you did take some telephone calls?"

"Oh, they asked for Lieutenant Fletcher," Tony said, "and that impressed Mrs. Berkowitz." He chuckled. "If you think you're mad, you should have seen Skeezix James. She wouldn't let him talk to me either. He had to come down in person."

"I'm trying to translate you in civilian English," Barbara said, "without much success."

"I'm in the reserve," he said. "I fly choppers. You have to 'stay current,' in other words, do a certain amount of flying, or else they make you go through another course, a repeater course. If I put in a couple of hours this weekend, at the Army Airfield at Lakehurst, I will have 'kept current.' Since I have to go to Jersey anyway, I thought it might be fun for you to come with me."

"Why not?" she said, as much to herself as to him.

7

Tony picked her up very early on Sunday morning. He was wearing a tieless uniform shirt, uniform pants and shoes, and when she got in the car, she saw a plastic clothesbag and decided that the rest of his uniform must be in that.

He told her, with satisfaction, that they'd worked until seven-thirty at the office, and then been up until almost midnight at the photo-processing plant waiting for the film to be developed and printed, and then running it.

"I think it's going to be all right," he said.

She asked him where he got the car, a red Corvette, and he told her he had rented it.

"Before I went in the army, I used to do Corey Rubber," he said. "The firm used to give me a car. A Morgan. Those were the good old days."

"Why this? It must have cost a fortune to rent."

"I'm trying to make an impression on a blonde," he said shamelessly.

Barbara wasn't very familiar with New Jersey, and she didn't like the idea of driving the Corvette, so she asked Tony to drop her at the beach before he went to the airfield, and to pick her up when he was finished flying.

Once he'd driven off, with a chirp of tires and a blat of the exhaust, she regretted again her decision to go with him. She didn't like the idea of being alone, and it didn't take long for her worst suspicions to be confirmed.

Any female, a good-looking one, alone on the beach, was assumed to be looking for masculine company. She hadn't been on the beach thirty minutes before a couple of clowns moved their blanket near hers and began to demonstrate their skill with a football.

She finally had to run them off, after a half hour of polite but increasingly firm rebuttal of their attentions. Then a girl spoke to her.

"The nice thing about this beach," she said, "is that they're like streetcars."

"I beg your pardon?" Barbara asked.

"The men come by like streetcars," the girl said. "You just have to wait until you see something you like."

"I'm meeting somebody," Barbara said.

"So are we all, we hope," the girl said, undaunted. Then: "Hey, look, a helicopter!"

"That's probably my boyfriend," Barbara said, the words slipping out before she really had a chance to consider them. She got a look of disbelief from the girl, and turned her attention to the helicopter.

It was a big one, one she remembered was called The Huey, whatever that meant.

It was coming down the beach, from the direction of Asbury Park, several hundred yards out to sea, and two hundred feet above the water. It flew somehow purposefully, and Barbara decided she had been absolutely wrong about it being Tony Fletcher.

But then, just past her, it made a sudden turn out to sea, seeming to slow down, and dropped even lower. It made almost a complete turn, and then headed straight for the beach, straight for her. Right over her, it soared skyward, and then turned out to sea again. It made another slow approach down the beach, and as she watched, a door in the fuselage opened, and a man in a helmet and flight suit stood in the door and waved gaily.

She fought, and then gave into the temptation to wave back. She got to her feet and waved, and, as if in reply, the pilot of the machine rocked it back and forth. It made one more pass, first going out to sea, and then coming in fast and low right at her. Then it gained altitude and flew inland and was seen no more.

It probably wasn't Tony after all, she decided, thinking that she'd made a fool of herself. It was just a combination of a helicopter and girls on a beach. Pilots waved at all girls, and, she supposed, all girls waved back. She felt like a fool.

The girl who had spoken to her made it worse.

"Hey," she called. "Has your friend got a friend?"

There was no possible reply she could make to that, so she pretended she didn't hear it, and instead got up, took her jacket off and ran into the surf. It was the temperature of ice water, and she couldn't stand it long. She

89

came out of the water and wrapped her towel around her and sat there for a long time trying to get warm.

It was almost two, and she was more than a little hungry, before Tony returned. At first (although, she thought, it must be Tony) she didn't recognize him. He was wearing a uniform cap now and a tunic and a necktie, and there were wings and a double row of ribbons on his breast pocket. He looked like an officer, and she was annoyed with herself. Tony had been—*was*—an officer, and she should have expected him to look like it.

Barbara was human enough to be pleased when she saw the girl who had spoken to her looking at Tony with fascination.

"Was that you waving?" Barbara asked.

"I was driving," Tony said. "Tom Agostino was waving. We're going to meet him for lunch, if that's all right with you. We were together in Vietnam."

"Fine," Barbara said. "Where is he?"

"He and some of the others have got a bachelor pad in Spring Lake," he said. "They're off buying clams and lobsters. I figured maybe you'd like that better than getting all dressed up and going to a restaurant."

"You're all dressed up," she said. "You look like a general."

"Just a lieutenant," he said. "And as soon as I get to their hootch, off this comes."

"Hootch?"

"House," he said. "They speak GI."

She had never been around soldiers before, and she didn't know what to expect, but what she got wasn't at all

90

what she thought it would be. When they reached the house, a rambling, huge old barn of a place just across the highway from the beach, it looked far more like a fraternity house than something to do with the military. No one was in uniform except Tony, and he changed to slacks and a sports shirt just as soon as he could. There seemed to be a firm, if unwritten, rule that the army or anything about it, was not a fit subject for conversation.

There were eight pilots, all bachelors, who shared the house, and there seemed to be (she didn't actually count) more girls around than bachelors. The house originally had been a rich man's summer house, complete with tennis court. That had deteriorated, but a higher net had been put up, and it was now a volleyball court. They played, Tony included, with enthusiasm, and when they finally wore out, they turned to food. The girls were waited on by the men, who boiled lobsters and corn and steamed clams. Barbara had just decided that this was a much nicer arrangement than having the gentler sex do all the kitchen work when she learned of another house rule. The men cooked, the women cleaned up.

They were clever people, solid people, *nice* people, and the afternoon went by pleasantly and quickly. When it was dark, Tony said his good-byes, and they got into the Corvette and drove back to New York City.

Barbara was told, as they left, that she was welcome anytime, with or without Russian Joe.

In the car on the Jersey Turnpike, Tony talked about them as soldiers. She was surprised to learn that Tom Agostino, a redheaded Italian, the one who had waved at her from the door of the helicopter, the one who had seemed to be the least military of any of them, was in fact the senior officer, a captain, a professional soldier and West Point graduate, who had been Tony's commanding officer in Vietnam.

"Did you ever think about staying in the army?" Barbara asked, from simple curiosity.

"The last couple of hours, I have," Tony said. "I may be looking for a job this time tomorrow."

"How do you mean that? Oh—the new campaign?"

"Uh huh."

"You're worried about it?"

"I'm so pleased with it," Tony said, "so sure that it would be a good one, one that would make people think of Brisk in the drugstore, and at the same time keep them from wincing when they see the commercials, that I'm worried."

"Why?"

"If it's good, how come somebody a lot smarter than me hasn't thought of it before?"

"You're supposed to be the Boy Wonder," Barbara said. "I'm sure Mr. James will like it."

"I can always become a professional chopper driver," he said. "Some of it's not so bad. Don't tell them I said so, but I miss those guys. They're good people."

"Yes, they are," she said. She also thought, but of course did not say, that she thought Tony Fletcher was pretty good people, too.

When Tony went to the projection room, a sort of small theatre outfitted with a table and some armchairs as well as a couple of rows of theatre seats, he was surprised to find Mr. Cantarella and Gibbons had been invited.

He wasn't happy about this. He had purposely pointed out that what he had was a very rough-cut film, thinking that Skeezix James would not want to show the clients anything but a far more refined project. What Tony had hoped to get from Skeezix was both the necessary money and the permission to make one 60-second commercial, plus a film/story board presentation of half a dozen or more, all following the new slant.

He had hoped, in other words, to have Cantarella judge a professional, polished, finished commercial, rather than what he had in the film can, which was just a shade more detailed than a rough story board.

There was nothing to do now but plunge ahead.

"Frankly, I hadn't expected to see you here," Tony began, smiling.

"You were, you know, supposed to keep me posted," Gibbons said, with a smile that Tony thought deserved some sort of prize for insincerity. "I was beginning to think you'd forgotten that."

"I didn't have anything to show you," Tony said. "You can consider this, if you like, being kept posted."

"If you've put it on film," Cantarella said reasonably, "you must be pretty well along, as well as pretty sure you're on the right track."

"This was shot—in my office, by the way—on an Auricon. It's very definitely not a finished film. If you would, please consider this as sort of a moving story-board, rather than anything like a finished product."

"OK, Tony," Cantarella said. "Let's see it."

"It comes with a speech, first," Tony said. "A brief one. My theory is that while people admit they use deodorant, they don't—at least I don't—like to be told how badly they smell without it. I also don't think that people really believe that all the good-looking girls in the world are going to come running after us, just because we went *psssst* with the spray can."

"You'd be surprised, Fletcher," Gibbons said, "how much Brisk we've sold telling people they do smell, and suggesting their romantic life will be somewhat broader if they—pssst—with Brisk."

The remark was unnecessary. Everyone in the room knew to within a couple of cases how much Brisk had been sold in each month of the past two years. It was designed to make Tony seem smart-aleck critical of a proven success, and it succeeded. There was nothing to do but ignore Gibbons.

"I hope this will have a tinge of subtle humor," Tony said. "I'm sure that if we had professional directors to shoot it, and refined the copy somewhat, we could accomplish this."

"You're not, I hope, going to laugh at Brisk?" Gibbons said.

"No, I'm not," Tony said. "The basic idea of this one rough-cut commercial, and the others that might possibly follow, is twofold. First, unspoken, that Brisk is necessary, and second, 'Don't Forget the Brisk.' "

"Roll the film, why don't you?" Gibbons said. "Let us figure it out for ourselves."

94

"Roll it, Bill," Tony said to Bill Lewis, and the room lights dimmed and the film flashed on the screen. It showed an attache case, open. A hand threw in socks, and then a shirt, and then ties, and then a manila folder lettered "MEETING AGENDA, REGIONAL MEETING, HOTEL FOUNTAINBLEAU, MIAMI, FLORIDA." The suitcase was closed and picked up, and then a voice said, "Ooops." The case was laid down again, and opened, and first a first-class airplane ticket was tossed in, and then a can of Brisk. A voice said, "Couldn't forget that," and then there was a shot of a jet liner taking off.

The screen flashed white as a strip of leader film ran past the projector bulb, and then an even rougher commercial came on. This showed two pieces of luggage. One was a large and obviously expensive shotgun case, containing an expensive shotgun. Beside it was an overnight bag. The camera picked up the program for Grand National Trapshoot at Vandalia, Ohio. A hand finished loading boxes of shotgun shells, then a pair of leather gloves, a pair of shooting glasses, a shooting jacket with an All-American Trap Team patch on it. Both cases were snapped shut, and then a voice said, "Ooops" and the overnight bag was reopened so a can of Brisk could be added to the other contents, and then the voice said. "Couldn't forget that."

There were four other variations of the same idea: One implied that the Brisk user who almost—but not quite —forgot his Brisk . . . was a deep sea sport fisherman; another that the Brisk user was a pilot of an intercontinental jet airliner; a third implied that the Brisk user was a professional baseball player and the last suggested that a just elected member of the Congress had almost, but not quite, forgotten the can of Brisk he couldn't do without on Capitol Hill.

It didn't take long. If the commercials were produced for use, they would run a precise 60 seconds. Some of the rough-cut commercials Tony had made ran over this time, and one was a few seconds under a minute. In just about five minutes, in other words, it was over. This was time enough for Tony to develop doubts, and then—he hoped objectively—to dispel them. These weren't bad, he thought. They weren't likely to win any prizes, but, all things considered, they weren't bad. They were fresh, and they seemed to serve their purpose, which was, in the final analysis, to sell Brisk deodorant.

The lights went on. Tony looked at Gibbons. The face he was making was that of a man who had just seen something distasteful, perhaps bordering on the obscene, and which he was doing his best, as a gentleman, to ignore. Tony looked at Mr. Cantarella. Cantarella met his eyes and shook his head sadly. Tony looked at Skeezix James. James shrugged his shoulders and raised his hands palm upward in a gesture of futility.

"Is this some kind of a joke, Fletcher?" Gibbons asked. "Another manifestation of that odd sense of humor of yours, or are you seriously proposing we actually put something like this out on the boob tube?"

"I didn't intend it as a joke," Tony said.

"I'm afraid not, Fletcher," Cantarella said. "Not at all. I just can't see that sort of thing." He looked at his watch.

96

"When you come up with something else, let's have a look at it. In the future, why don't you work a little more closely with Bob Gibbons? So that he could at least point you in the right direction?"

"I would have shot this down, the moment it stuck its head out of the sand," Gibbons said.

"Yes, I'm sure you would have," Tony said.

"Let's go, Bob," Cantarella said. "Sorry, Skeezix."

Neither said a word of farewell to Tony Fletcher.

"And now," James said, when they were gone, "words to rank in the history of man—back to the drawing board, Tony."

"Skeezix," Tony said. "That's it."

"I don't follow you," James said.

"I thought that was pretty good," Tony said. "Not perfect. But a beginning."

"You got voted down, sport, three to one," James said. "That just won't do."

"That's all I've got," Tony said.

"Don't be absurd," James said, somewhat sharply.

"I'm not being absurd," Tony said. "I didn't want this job in the first place, and I told you that. When you insisted, I did the best job I knew how to do. I'm sorry—but not really surprised—that it didn't meet with approval. But that's all there is, Skeezix. I'm what is known as dry."

"You're in the advertising business," James said. "You're not allowed to get dry. I'll tell you what: You spend the day chewing this over in your mind, and then, either last thing this afternoon, or first thing in the morning, we'll brainstorm it together."

"And what," Tony said, "if I can't come up with something?"

"Then, maybe, you're in the wrong business, sport," James said, and he said it with a smile, but Tony didn't like the threat any more because of the smile.

Tony went back to his office and tried very hard to think of another approach. He told himself that he was supposed to be an advertising man, and that, therefore, he should have a whole line of alternative ideas. He had none.

Mrs. Berkowitz came into the office.

"You had two telephone calls, Mr. Fletcher," she said. "I told them you couldn't be disturbed."

"Who were they?"

"Mr. Gibbons called," she said, "and a Mr. Parten."

"What did Gibbons want?"

"He asks that you call back and make an appointment with his secretary, so that you can go into your problem."

"Oh," Tony said. That meant that Gibbons was pressing his advantage. He was summoning Tony to his office, at his convenience, so that the errant and somewhat backward delinquent could be put on the straight and narrow path. "Who's Parten?" Tony asked.

"I don't know," Mrs. Berkowitz said. "He left his number and asked that you call him when you have a free minute." She laid the number on his desk and left the room.

He returned to his study of the windows in the adjacent building, and to his frustrating and fruitless search

98

for fresh ideas on how to sell deodorant, but this latest telephone call wouldn't leave his mind.

Finally, he turned around and dialed the number. It was probably something awful, but it would be best to have all the walls fall in now, rather than have one waiting to fall on him later.

"Stu Parten," a very cordial—overcordial—voice said.

"My name is Fletcher, Mr. Parten," Tony said. "I'm returning your call."

"Very good of you, Mr. Fletcher. Thank you for calling back so quickly."

"What can I do for you, Mr. Parten?"

"It is not a question of what you can do for me, but of what I can do for you, and you can do for yourself."

"I don't need any insurance," Tony said. "If that's what this is all about."

"I'm not selling anything, Fletcher," Parten said. "Except maybe you."

"I wish you'd get to the point, Mr. Parten," Tony said. "I've had a bad morning, and I'm in no mood for playing Twenty Questions."

"All right," Parten said. "I'm a pirate."

"I beg your pardon?"

"Or a body snatcher. Take your pick."

"Look—" Tony said impatiently.

"I know somebody who knows all about you, Fletcher," Parten said. "Somebody is very impressed with you."

"You've been talking to my grandfather?"

"No, and I can't tell you who I've been talking to. Just yet."

99

"You've just been talking to me," Tony said, "and now the game is over."

"How would you like a twenty per cent raise?" Parten said quickly.

"Just fine," Tony said. "But I don't think my prospects are too good for a raise, just now."

"Having a little trouble over there, are you? Fine."

"You've got thirty seconds to start making sense," Tony said.

"I have a client who is familiar with the work you did for Corey Rubber and for Blackman Boats," Parten said. "It's one of the Big Ten in the advertising industry, and *their* client is an AAAA-rated manufacturer of sporting goods. They want a whole new slant on their whole advertising program, and they want you on the team."

"As what?"

"Chief copywriter for openers, and if you can hack it, account executive for the client in three months."

"Wow," Tony said. "You sure you got the right guy?"

"I'm sure. You interested?"

"I've got a job," Tony said.

"Whatever you're making, plus twenty per cent, plus another twenty per cent in three months if you stay on as chief copywriter. If you become the account executive, more than that, of course. But that much guaranteed."

"Well, I—"

"Don't jump, either way," Parten said. "You think about it overnight, and you call me tomorrow, all right? You've got the number. Think carefully," Parten concluded. "The name of this game is money."

The phone went dead. Tony took the instrument from his ear and looked at it.

He was astonished. His first reaction was that it was simply out of the question, that he was a Collier, Richards employee and would remain one. But then it ceased being that simple. He had just laid an enormous egg, at least according to James, Cantarella and Gibbons. He had just been ordered to do something he knew he simply couldn't do. He was absolutely out of ideas for deodorant.

At that moment, a couple of irreverent ideas popped into his head. One showed one of the normal, too handsome, male models standing beside one of the normal, too beautiful female models. She was holding her nose and making a face. There would just be a few words of copy: "LESS RISK WITH BRISK."

Another one, even less reverent. A standard advertising family, too handsome and wholesome and happy to possibly be for real. Momma, Poppa, and a half-dozen sickeningly sweet youngsters. The copy here would be "THE FAMILY THAT SPRAYS TOGETHER STAYS TOGETHER."

Tony decided that he was ethically bound to tell Skeezix James of the offer of employment. He thought, too, that maybe hearing about it would make Skeezix think twice, and take him off this assignment and give him something to do that he had the experience and the qualifications and the enthusiasm to do well.

He went to the drawing board and sketched out his ideas, working rapidly and well. Then he sat down at his typewriter and typed an interoffice memorandum:

(1) Herewith my fresh ideas for Brisk. I hope they will be more in keeping with what the sage of Deodorant, Mr. Gibbons, has in mind.

(2) I had a rather interesting telephone call from a man who identified himself as a body snatcher and offered me, ultimately, 40% more money than I'm making here to do a campaign for sporting goods for an unidentified competitor. He wouldn't let me tell him "no," or even what a loyal employee I am.

(3) Isn't there something around here besides this that I could do to earn my keep?

Regards,
Tony

He had Mrs. Berkowitz get him a large envelope, and then called for a messenger to have it delivered to Mr. James's office. He told the messenger to stick around to wait for a reply. The messenger returned with the information that Mr. James was out of the office, was not expected back for the balance of the day, and that he had left the material with the secretary.

It was quarter after three. Tony could see no point in sticking around the office. He had nothing to do, and he had, working nights and on Saturday, accumulated a great deal more of what the company called compensatory time than the hour and forty-five minutes remaining in the day.

He called Barbara, and said he'd meet her at the Deli for an early supper at six, and afterwards they'd do whatever she wanted to do.

"It didn't go well, huh?"

"No, ma'am," he said. "That's something of an under-statement."

"It'll turn out all right, Tony," Barbara said. "You just wait and see."

He very much appreciated her loyalty, even though he was quite sure she was dead wrong.

8

There was an interoffice memorandum lying on his desk when he came to work the next morning. From the look of concern in Mrs. Berkowitz' eyes, he knew that she had read it.

1. Frankly, I found your "wit" both juvenile and in very bad taste.

2. As frankly, I was offended by the thinly veiled threat your rather transparent, imagined, offer of employment elsewhere implied.

3. The normal working hours, as you should by now know, at this firm are 9 to 5. In the future, if you find it necessary to leave your office before normal quitting time, you are to ask my permission first.

4. Please present yourself at my office at your earliest free moment so that we may discuss both the Brisk campaign and your future with the firm in some detail.

S. James
Vice-President, Creativity

The blood, as Tony read James's memorandum, drained from his face. Then the unpleasant feeling in the pit of his stomach, the embarrassment and the knowledge that he had been misunderstood were replaced by old-fashioned fury. James had as much as called him a liar, and that was difficult to take from anyone, much less someone you had considered your friend. That crack about taking off early was unfair. Not only did the company owe him the time, three or four or five times over, but it would have been impossible for him to ask permission to leave of someone who wasn't available.

There was only one possible answer to the problem, and it suggested itself immediately, and that was to quit. Tony knew himself well enough to force himself not to jump to a hasty action. He drank two cups of coffee, and tried his best to think of alternatives to quitting. He could think of none. James was obviously determined to keep him on the deodorant account, and James had just as obviously decided he was juvenile, possessed of bad taste, and untrustworthy.

Tony sat down at his typewriter and wrote out a short letter of resignation. He was on the verge of calling for a messenger to deliver it, but then decided he would deliver it himself. He didn't want James to get the idea that he was afraid of him, and running, and it seemed very important that he let James know the offer of employment elsewhere was not a product of his imagination.

He folded the resignation neatly in thirds, put it into his inside jacket pocket and went to Skeezix James's office.

"Mr. Fletcher to see Mr. James," he said to the secretary.

"I'm sorry, he asked not to be disturbed," she said.

"Tell him I'm here, please," Tony said. "I think he expects me."

She shrugged her shoulders and pushed the intercom lever.

"Mr. Fletcher to see you, Mr. James," she chirped.

"You tell Mr. Fletcher to wait," the voice came back, "and try to remember the next time that when I say I don't want to be disturbed, I really don't want to be disturbed."

"You see?" the secretary said to Tony. "I told you."

"I'll wait," Tony said. He wondered what would happen if he just walked in. He decided that James would simply consider that another manifestation of his juvenile attitudes and bad taste. He would wait, and then, according to Hoyle, he would quit. He picked up a copy of *Advertising Age* from the coffee table and slumped down in the chair.

Five minutes later, a short, bald-headed, trim little man, deeply tanned, came into the office. He called to Tony's mind a bantam rooster.

"Is James in?" he asked.

"Yes, he is," the secretary said, "but—"

"That's an improvement," the little man said. "Yesterday afternoon, he was off somewhere, pursuing the muse."

A man after my own heart, Tony decided.

106

"And today he's in there in solitary splendor," Tony offered. "Contemplating his navel."

"Is that so?" the little man said, and smiled. "I can't say I'm surprised. Tell him that Garrett is out here, honey, and that he'll have to check his navel on his own time."

"Mr. James does not wish to be disturbed," the secretary said.

"I told you," Tony said. "When she announced me, he practically bit her head off."

"That's roughly what I've got in mind," the little man said. He came over and sat beside Tony on the couch. "You're first in line, apparently," he said. "Is what you've got to do going to take long?"

"Not more than 90 seconds or so," Tony said. "I'm just going in there to tell him I've quit."

"I may take a little longer, but we're on the same sort of business," the little man said. "I'm going to tell him he's fired."

"Oh?" Tony asked.

"I'm going to tell him," the little man said, raising his voice for the secretary's benefit, "that unless he can come up with something fresh, like yesterday, that the Seneca Division of Amalgamated Motors is going to go elsewhere for its advertising."

Mr. James's new secretary was not stupid. She pushed the intercom and said, "Mr. James, Mr. Garrett is here and wants to see you."

"I thought I had the magic words," Garrett said to Tony with a smile of triumph.

107

James's door flew open and Skeezix came out, hand extended, smiling broadly.

"Hello, Pete," he said. "Good to see you. I hope Tony kept you amused while you were waiting."

"He's a regular comic," Garrett said. "Funny, funny. I understand he's first in line."

James wanted to change the subject. "What's on your mind, Pete?" he asked.

"You and I, Skeezix, ol' buddy, are going to look at some film. And then you're going to tell me whether you think they're as bad as I do, or whether they're just plain lousy."

"Oh, come on, Pete," James said. "They can't be as bad as that."

"That, ol' buddy, is what you think. I suppose you *do* have a projector around?"

"Tony, would you run down and arrange for a projectionist right away while I get Mr. Garrett a cup of coffee and some happy pills?"

"Don't you want to hear what he has to say?" Garrett asked. "That may brighten your whole day, too."

"After you and I are finished," James said smoothly.

Tony was already on his way for the projector. He regretted running off at the mouth. James was obviously right; he was juvenile. While nothing had changed that would make him want to reconsider his decision to resign, it was common decency to keep the affair away from the clients, and he hadn't done that.

He could make some small amends by keeping his

mouth shut from here on in, and by running to get a projector.

By the time he returned to the office, Skeezix had unrolled a projection screen which was normally hidden in a wall of his office, and had rolled out a table for the projector to sit on. Garrett and he were sitting in two armchairs, waiting for the motion pictures to be shown.

Tony set the projector up, threaded the film and decided that he had no further business in the room.

"It's ready to roll, Mr. James," he said. "I'll leave, and you can shut it off when you're ready."

"Stick around," Garrett said. "You may learn something. And you can play the role of John Q. Public for Skeezix here."

Tony looked at James, and James nodded. Tony shut off the lights, and started the camera.

Although the film was a good deal more professional looking than the one Tony had made, it was still what is known in the advertising business as a rough-cut. When it was eventually completed, edited carefully, the level of the light and of the sound evened out and made smooth, it would be one major part—the important part—of the Seneca Motor Car Division's television advertising campaign. It was designed for the Seneca Firebrand, the fast, (and expensive) "personal" car, near the top of the Seneca line, and the one, Tony knew, that carried what is known as the Seneca "image." All the other (cheaper) cars were almost as fast, or flashy, as the Firebrand.

As Tony watched it, he thought that it wasn't the most

109

original advertising campaign he had ever seen. It was the fairly standard practice of connecting the product with someone high up in sports. In this case, the two dozen commercials they watched for half an hour were repetitions of the same theme. A Firebrand would roar at the camera, and then there would be a long shot of the car as it came off the track at Daytona International Speedway. The camera moved in for a medium closeup of the car, then for a tight shot of the face of the driver, a professional racing driver. The drivers then rolled down the window and announced that as they loved the Firebrand on the track, they loved it off the track as well, and chose it for their personal transportation.

By the time they had seen all the commercials with only the face of the driver changing, Tony was embarrassed and uncomfortable. It was not, by any means, the greatest TV campaign Collier, Richards had ever put out. It was almost as bad as the Brisk commercials.

"If I were connected with neither your fine organization," Garrett said icily, "nor my fine organization, and were just a simple potential customer watching my television set, you know what I would think?"

There was an uncomfortable silence, and then Garrett went on: "I would think that you went down to that racetrack, and paid that guy to read that commercial. It would not inspire me to rush out and buy a Firebrand."

There was more silence.

Garrett turned to Tony. "Since you tell me you are about to be an ex-employee, and may therefore be objective, is that a fair assessment?"

110

"Yes, sir," Tony said. "It is. But it's only a rough cut, and I'm sure it can be—"

"How would you do it, my unemployed young friend?"

"You've got me on a spot," Tony said.

"Tell him, Tony," James said. "I hate to agree with him, but he's right. It didn't look that bad on the story board, or in the pre-production conferences. What would you do?"

"I'd put the emphasis on the car," Tony said. "Just identify the driver briefly. Most of them are famous enough anyway, with just an underline to rub it in. Show them briefly, and then show the car." He paused. He was afraid he was sounding like a wise guy.

"Is that all you can think of?" Garrett asked nastily, and that was enough to get Tony started again.

"No," he said. "It isn't. I'd cover the races, hoping that the Firebrand would win. When it did, I'd do a couple of 60-second and 90-second newsreel type shots of the race and show them that same week. If they didn't win, I'd have a bunch of pit area, garage area, that kind of thing, backup commercials, showing a street model Firebrand parked next to a racing model."

He stopped; he had gone too far again, and he felt twice embarrassed. Once for making a fool of himself and again for embarrassing Skeezix James.

Garrett finally got to his feet.

"Just between us boys, Skeezix," Garrett said. "A kid who is about to quit has come up in thirty seconds with a better idea than that commercial. I expect to see a new idea in forty-eight hours in Detroit."

111

He walked out of the room.

"Ouch," Skeezix said, as he closed the door after him. "That is what is known as getting your nose bent."

"I'm sorry I ran off at the mouth again," Tony said. "But he *asked*—"

Skeezix ignored him. "Aside from a camera crew, including a director, what are you going to need?"

"Huh?"

"I'll have to send somebody down to the lab to personally supervise the souping and the printing," James went on. "I think you'd better do two, with different sets and actors, each time. One, winning a race, and one in the shop."

"What are you talking about?"

"He said forty-eight hours, and he means forty-eight hours, and in forty-eight hours he's going to be looking at a finish-cut version of a pair of demonstration commercials," Skeezix said.

"And you want me to do it?" Tony asked. "Do you know how many films I've made? I thought it was generally agreed that I'm incompetent." James ignored him. When he did, Tony asked, "Aside from my brilliant success with Brisk?"

"No."

"None."

"You can do it. I'll get you the best crew available."

The look on Skeezix' face was friendly and enthusiastic; it was the sort of look Tony remembered before having gone into the army. He hadn't seen it lately.

"I came up here to quit," Tony said.

112

"So you were saved by the bell," James said. "Let it go at that."

"It's not that easy. I may have been guilty of bad taste —I'm not sure—about the funny drawings for Brisk, but I wasn't putting you on about the offer of a job. That was bona fide, and I don't like being told I'm a liar."

"OK, I apologize," James said. "Satisfied?"

"I don't know," Tony said.

"You're not holding me up for more money, are you, Tony?" James asked thoughtfully. "Because if you are, forget it. You're making more now, frankly, than you've earned."

"I'm not asking for a raise," Tony said. "And because I apparently blew it with the Brisk business, I'll do the best I can with the Firebrand commercials. And I have to tell you that I figure the company owes me a whole lot more compensatory time than the hour and forty-five minutes I took yesterday."

"You know what?" James asked, and then went on without waiting for a reply. "I get mad, too. Just like human beings. When I saw those too, too clever charcoal sketches of yours, I got mad. This is a business, not a college humor magazine. I got mad and I snapped out at you. You were wrong, and I was wrong, and this is what my mother used to call a chance to start clean on a fresh page."

He put out his hand. Tony took it.

"Yes, sir," he said.

They went to LaGuardia Field in a hired limousine, which was not nearly as luxurious as it sounds, and was

113

actually a very practical solution to the problem. For one thing, they couldn't have loaded all the equipment they were taking with them into a taxi, but the equipment and their luggage fitted into the limousine's trunk, and in the space in the back seat over the folded-down jump seats.

There were five people. There was a director, a man in his middle forties who seemed to be perfectly willing to take orders from someone Tony's age. There was a cameraman and his assistant, and a sound man and his assistant, and there was a sound man and a general all-around assistant called a grip.

Mrs. Berkowitz had called around and found that a race was being run at Daytona, and somehow she'd managed to find them rooms at a motel. Skeezix James had called the track officials himself, and greased their path there. They would be expected. He told Tony that he should contact the head of the Seneca Firebrand Racing Team when he got there, and that by the time he got there, he would have called Detroit so that the racing team, too, would be expecting the film crew.

Tony stopped by personnel and picked up expense money, $2,000, more cash than he had ever before carried. When the crew met outside the building, after having made quick trips either home or to clothing stores for a change of clothes, and they had loaded the limousine with the equipment and their luggage, they stopped by Tony's apartment while he rushed upstairs and threw a change of clothing into a suitcase.

114

They reached the airport with ten minutes to spare before the plane left. Tony, slightly shocked, signed the bill for the tickets and the excess luggage. This was going to be a very expensive excursion.

9

There was no direct service to Daytona Beach. They flew to Miami and had forty-five minutes between planes there. This gave Tony enough time to call Daytona, where a pleasant masculine voice told him that he'd just heard from Detroit, and that the red carpet was in the process of being rolled out. Was there anything he could do?

"Could you call the Hertz people and reserve a couple of station wagons for us?" Tony asked.

"Be glad to. I'll meet your plane, Mr. Fletcher."

"Thanks very much," Tony said. When he hung up, he saw that he still had thirty minutes before the Daytona plane left. He called Barbara at her office.

"How did it go?" she asked.

"Like a Swiss watch," he said. "They're going to meet us at the airport."

"Who's meeting whom at what airport?"

"I'm in Miami," he said. "On my way to Daytona."

116

"What I was asking, in my innocence, was about the Brisk commercials," Barbara said.

"Oh, that. Well, I almost quit and I almost got fired, but that's all over. I'm doing a rush job on a Firebrand commercial for the Seneca Motors account. I'll tell you all about it when I get back."

"When will that be?"

"I ought to leave Daytona tomorrow night for Detroit," he said. "Day after tomorrow."

"My," she said. "Don't we get around!"

"What are you sore about?" he asked.

"I was all upset about you and the Brisk commercials, and here it is, already ancient history," Barbara said.

"Just keep holding your breath," Tony said. "This could be just as much of a disaster as that was."

"Behave yourself," she said.

The next day and a half passed very quickly, with little time for sleep. It was just getting dark as they reached Daytona, and as soon as they'd checked into a motel, they went out to the Daytona International Speedway. James had suggested using actors. Tony decided that there simply wasn't time to find actors and then to teach them what was needed. Furthermore, the whole flavor of the commercials would be changed if actors were used.

They spent the night making motion pictures of the Firebrand work area and pit area. The pictures would have a newsreel, rather than studio, quality, but Tony thought that this would be an asset rather than a liability. Just after midnight, the grip, an amiable Frenchman known as Frenchy, naturally, was dispatched with four

117

cans of film in one of the station wagons to Jacksonville, where he would arrange to get the film on an early morning flight to Detroit. That much time could be saved, by having that much film processed while they were taking pictures of the race.

At five o'clock in the morning, before first light, they were back at the Speedway. They were able to film the last of the speed trials, and then the beginning of the race. After he set up the large Mitchell camera where it would be used to film the race itself, and a smaller Bell & Howell at the pit—where, hopefully, the winner would return triumphantly after the race, the head cameraman took a hand-held Eyemo camera and prepared to take pictures of the race from a helicopter while the race was in progress.

Tony was tempted to fly the helicopter himself, but decided against it in the interests of maturity. He was down here to supervise the operation, not fly.

The Seneca Division of the Amalgamated Motors Company had entered three Seneca Firebrands in the race. They were driven by professionals whose interest was in winning the race, not in posing for pretty pictures for a television commercial.

One of them, made nervous by the poking of the camera lens and microphone, told Tony so in no uncertain terms. Tony called the crew off. In the long run, anything that interfered with the Firebrands' chances of winning, no matter how good a commercial it would make, was wrong.

The assistant sound man was pressed into service run-

118

ning the Bell & Howell camera in the pits; the grip assisted the Mitchell camera operator, and Tony Fletcher was left without anything to do. He realized that he really wasn't needed.

The race began at 1:30 in the afternoon. Two hours and five minutes later, the 300-mile race was over; a Seneca Firebrand had come in first; and they had footage of the race, the end of the race, and of the smiling, grease-bedecked driver being handed the trophy and the check.

Tony by then was ready to go. He had his bag packed, and one of the station wagons gassed and ready to drive to Tampa, across the peninsula, where he and the head cameraman would catch a plane to Detroit. The head cameraman would serve as editor, once the film had been developed and printed in the Detroit laboratories of Collier, Richards & Company.

He managed to get a little sleep on the plane, but there was no sleep at all that night once they got to Detroit. It wasn't that he was especially needed. The head cameraman had long years of experience in the business, knew what Tony was after, agreed with the idea, and was wholly able to do the cutting and the splicing himself. Tony, however, didn't think it would be right if he went to sleep while asking someone else to spend the night working. He stayed up, and tried to make himself as useful, and unobtrusive, as possible.

By half past nine the next morning, the final cut was finished. It took Tony about fifteen minutes to write the narrator's speech, and by eleven, an announcer had recorded the narration, it had been joined with the film,

119

and there was, as the net result of the effort of at least a dozen people working around the clock for a day and a half, a completed 60-second commercial, suitable, Tony hoped, for television broadcast.

At twelve o'clock, freshly shaved, but wearing what he knew were travel-mussed clothes, and in the company of a Mr. Crosby, the Seneca Motors Division account executive, a gray-haired, distinguished-appearing gentleman who was polite but distant to Tony, he presented himself in the office of Mr. Peter Garrett in the Amalgamated Motors Company Building.

"Well," Garrett said. "Look who's here. James made you put your money where your mouth is, did he?"

"Hello, Mr. Garrett," Tony said.

"You've come, I suppose, to tell me why it was impossible to do what I told you to do in that short a period of time?"

"We came to show it to you," Tony said. "The commercial, not the excuses."

"I'm impressed," Garrett said. "Let's eat first. That way it won't ruin my appetite."

They had a very good lunch in a very elegant dining room on the top floor of the building. Tony had a very hard time keeping from yawning. Garrett seemed to be aware of this, and amused by it.

Mr. Crosby, the account executive, managed to convey the impression that he had no responsibility for Tony, or what Tony did or had not done.

Tony drank four cups of coffee in an attempt to keep

120

awake. He was still sleepy, but all the coffee made his stomach churn audibly.

They went to a small projection room in the building, and Tony turned the film over to a projectionist. Garrett settled himself into a comfortable leather armchair, the account executive took the one beside it, and Tony was left standing up.

It was only the second time that Tony had seen the finished version. It was, considering the circumstances under which it had been made, very good. But it still looked rough.

The film began with an identifying shot, a few feet of a sign reading: DAYTONA INTERNATIONAL SPEEDWAY, and then a few more feet of a sign reading: FIREBRAND RACING TEAM. AUTHORIZED PERSONNEL ONLY.

The announcer's voice said: "Firebrand is engineered well, to run safely and fast." Now there was an interior shot of mechanics working on a Firebrand.

"This is the toughest testing ground in the world," the announcer's voice said, over a shot of the start of the race.

There was the high-pitched roar of cars passing by as the race went on.

"This week," the announcer said, "Firebrand engineering and Firebrand sturdiness were behind the Firebrand Win of the Magnolia 300 at Daytona International Speedway." There was a shot of the winning car passing the checkered flag, and then of the smiling, dirty driver getting the trophy and the check. Then there was a quick cut to a shot of a shining Firebrand racer sitting alone.

121

"First on the track," the announcer's voice said, and then, as a Firebrand convertible rolled up beside the racer, "and first on the road. *Firebrand!* See *your* dealer today!"

The screen went white. Garrett lit a long black cigar that looked even longer and blacker because he was so small.

"Well, Mr. Crosby," he asked, his voice giving away exactly nothing, "what is your professional opinion of that little bit of film?"

"It's difficult to say, Pete," Crosby said, very sincerely. "I think perhaps we—uh—that is, Skeezix and Tony here went into this a little hastily. There is, uh—certainly—some merit—"

"Answer the question," Garrett said impatiently. "Do you like it or don't you?"

There was a long pause, and then Crosby said, "Frankly, speaking frankly, just between us, that is. No. I can't say that I do. It's rough and uneven, and I don't think it sets up the—image—we're after."

"Frankly," Garrett said, mimicking him. "Speaking frankly, just between us, I think that sets up precisely the image we're after. What's wrong with winning? Even vicariously? I personally take a whole lot of pride in knowing that the car I make, and drive, is capable of taking something like the Magnolia 300."

"Well, of course, putting it that way—" Crosby began.

"Fletcher, how soon can we get that on the air?"

Tony had absolutely no idea what would be necessary to have the film put on television.

"I don't know, Mr. Garrett," he said. "I'll find out for you."

"No. That's Crosby's job," Garrett said. "You go make some more film. Crosby, you do what you have to do to get that on the air. I want it to replace 25% of the current schedule."

"Of course, Mr. Garrett," Crosby said. "I'll get right on it. Perhaps, since you've decided to go ahead with this, we'll be able, in the future, to have a little better quality film. Smoother, more polished."

"Then it will look like a commercial. The way it is, it looks like news. It is news. Just keep on doing what you did, Fletcher."

"Yes, sir."

"I'll work very closely with Fletcher on this, Mr. Garrett," Crosby said.

"Just so long as you don't mess up what he's doing," Garrett said. He stood up, looked at Tony, puffed on his cigar, said, "Thank you, gentlemen," and walked out of the room.

Tony looked at Crosby.

"What would you like me to do now, Mr. Crosby?" Tony asked.

"You better hop back to New York," Crosby said. "I'll be in touch with Mr. James, and we'll handle it that way."

"Yes, sir," Tony said. He didn't have to be an astute judge of human nature to see that Crosby was not overjoyed at Garrett's reception of the commercial. Tony saw himself as Crosby saw him, and that was as a threat to his

123

own role in the scheme of things, an intruder, more or less, who had pleased the client where he had failed.

Very tired, Tony collected his bag at the Detroit offices of Collier, Richards & Company and caught the next plane he could make back to New York. He went directly to his apartment, and decided that he would just rest his eyes a few minutes before calling either Skeezix or Barbara. He lay down on the bed in his underwear at quarter after seven, and slept through until ten o'clock the next morning.

When he got to the office at quarter to eleven, Mrs. Berkowitz greeted him with a relieved smile.

"I was worried about you," she said. "You just made it."

"Made what?"

"There's a conference in Mr. James's office in ten minutes. I called your apartment, but there was no answer."

"I overslept," Tony said. "I haven't had much sleep in the last couple of days."

"I'll bet," she said.

The conference convened in one of the meeting rooms at eleven o'clock. If Skeezix James had any idea that Tony had come into the building just a few minutes before, instead of at nine o'clock, he didn't say anything.

It was a full-scale conference, far larger than Tony had expected it to be. Crosby was there. Tony found out that the reason the conference was at eleven rather than first thing in the morning was to permit Crosby time to fly in from Detroit. With the exception of Tony and half a dozen secretaries who came to make notes, everyone present was a senior executive of Collier, Richards & Com-

124

pany. The Chief, Scheduling Division, was there, and the Director, Motion Picture Services. So was the Vice-President, Administration, (Barbara's boss, two or three times removed) and the Vice-President, Operations. The Chief Copywriter for the Seneca Account had flown in from Detroit with Crosby, bringing with him his two assistants, the man responsible for television and radio commercials and the man responsible for the preparation of advertisements for newspapers and magazines. Finally, there was the Corporate Counsel, although Tony wasn't quite sure what he would have to contribute.

The meeting was called to order by Skeezix James, who had effortlessly slipped from his normal, low-key, informal pattern of behavior into a pattern befitting Stanley S. James, Vice-President, Creativity, Member of the Board of Directors, and Chairman, Executive Committee of the firm.

The first order of business was a screening of the commercial Tony had just made. It was shown once, rewound, and then shown again.

"There is very little purpose in discussing the film we have just seen," James said. "Primarily, it is what the client asked for, what he got, and what he approved. I think Mr. Fletcher, and those who helped him, did a first-rate job in the time they had to work. Mr. Garrett told Mr. Crosby yesterday that he wanted this facet of the campaign to fill 25% of the time we have contracted for. He called me this morning to tell me that he had changed his mind, that he wants it to replace one-third of the schedule, and that he wants a similar percentage of

125

periodic media space so allocated. I think we may expect him to further raise those percentages to fifty per cent, and perhaps even higher, if it is as successful as he thinks it will be, and I have the opinion that it will be.

"The program, in other words, is settled. This conference is called to establish the procedures by which the program can be carried forth in the most efficient and economical manner possible."

Tony soon learned that he would no longer be responsible for directing the films to be made. The Director of Motion Picture Services would provide a full-time team, including a director. The film would be shot following a script prepared by Mr. Crosby's Chief Copywriter. The Director of Operations would arrange for the exposed film to be taken from the place where it had been shot and to have it processed, and to see that, after review by Mr. Crosby, it was delivered to the television networks so that it might be broadcast. The Director of Operations would also assume all responsibility for travel arrangements for the motion picture crews.

Everybody, Tony saw, had a role in this except the Corporate Counsel and one Anthony Fletcher.

Three hours after the conference had begun, just before it was adjourned, his name came up.

"Mr. Fletcher will continue to monitor the program, reporting directly to me," James said.

"Skeezix, don't you think that Mr. Fletcher should report to you through my shop?" Crosby asked.

"No. Your people can report to you. I want Tony to

126

stay on top of the whole thing, so that he can monitor the overall program." He smiled. "After all, this is his idea, you know." Crosby had attempted, and failed, to have Tony put under his thumb. But Tony was immediately aware that this was no sort of a victory for him. His duties had not been spelled out, nor had anything been said about his authority.

When the meeting was adjourned, he waited until he was alone with James and then brought this up.

"Now that we're friends again," he said, "can I ask a question?"

"What is it?" James replied, not returning Tony's smile.

"I sort of missed out on what I'm supposed to do," Tony said.

"You weren't asleep at the meeting," James said. "I looked."

"What exactly am I supposed to do?"

"Just what you were told to do," James said. "You're my eyes on the project."

"What am I supposed to be watching?"

"You know what Garrett wants," James said. "See that he gets it."

"I got the impression that Mr. Crosby and his people are in charge."

"They are."

"Then what if I see that what they are doing isn't what Mr. Garrett wants?"

"I'm sure it will be," James said. "But if it isn't, there's this remarkable invention. You pick it up, and you talk into it. They call it a telephone."

127

"I see."

"Don't make waves, Tony. You got your way. It looks to me like you'll have an interesting time during the racing season—and all of it on the expense account. Stop playing primadonna, will you?"

"I didn't mean to," Tony said. "Sorry."

"Watch what goes on. These are highly skilled, experienced, first class people. You can learn from them."

"Sure," Tony said, and forced a smile he did not feel. He was able to stop in time from saying what he was thinking, that first of all, he didn't think he was a trainee any more, and if he was, he was probably the highest paid apprentice in the world. Except, maybe, he thought, the Prince of Wales.

Barbara didn't share his concern when he bought dinner for her that night. So far as she was concerned, he was out of the mess with Brisk. Anything was better than that.

10

The next morning, there was an interoffice memorandum from Operations, telling him that the next film would be shot at the Darlington, S.C., Speedway, and in the same envelope was a round-trip airline ticket, an expense form, and a penciled telephone message saying that reservations had been confirmed for him at the Pines Motel.

He caught the plane that same afternoon. He didn't see any of the others on the plane, and when he finally reached Darlington and took a taxi from the airport to the motel, they weren't registered there, nor expected.

He decided that he probably was supposed to be sort of an advance man, so he called Hertz and ordered a rental car. He would go out to the track and arrange what he could before the others showed up.

"Would a Ford be all right, Mr. Fletcher?"

"Afraid not. I'll need a Seneca Firebrand," Tony said. "It really is the only car, you know."

Hertz didn't happen to have a Seneca Firebrand, so he rented, instead, a Seneca Expedition Stationwagon. When it was delivered, he drove out to the track and introduced himself to the track officials. Not only was he unexpected, but he found that everyone else was already here.

He was provided with Press credentials, a red tag to be tied to his buttonhole, which would permit him access both to the track itself and to the pit and garage areas as well. Apparently it had been decided in the upper echelons of NASCAR that NASCAR was getting a perfectly delightful free ride on the Seneca Firebrand advertising, and that it was only right that NASCAR make themselves as cooperative as possible.

He looked up the racing team and found, as he suspected he would, that the commercial filming operation was well under way, and was being performed by professionals who knew what they were doing and how to do it, and required virtually nothing from A. Fletcher, Esq.

After standing around feeling useless for about an hour, he went back to the motel, took a shower, checked again to make sure none of the others were in his motel, and then went into the bar for a glass of beer.

He was watching, with some fascination, a beer advertisement behind the bar which changed colors and shapes and looked the sort of thing a hypnotist might use, when two index fingers were suddenly, and with precision, jabbed into his rib cage under each arm. The intended result was effected. Tony practically jumped straight up off his stool.

130

"Well, as I live and breathe, if it isn't the Mad Russian himself," a familiar voice said. "How be ye, Lieutenant Fletcher?" He turned to look into the square, solid, suntanned face of Terry Boag.

"*Mr.* Boag," Tony said. "What's a disreputable bum like you doing in a nice place like this?"

They shook hands; they had last seen one another at an army airfield in Vietnam when it really had been Lieutenant Fletcher and Mr.—Warrant Officers are called Mister—Boag.

"Trying to earn an honest million as a race driver," Boag said. "Which, despite what you might have heard, is somewhat less risky than being a Huey driver. Don't tell me you're fascinated with racing, Tony? You don't strike me as the type."

"I didn't know you drove, Terry," Tony said. "Are you driving here? In the 500?"

"I'm driving here, but not in the 500," Terry Boag said. "I'm running in the preliminaries, so to speak. The modified 250-miler which comes before the big race. You didn't answer my question," Boag said, and then he reached into Tony's breast pocket and pulled out the red Press badge. "You're a reporter?"

"Not quite," Tony said, and explained his function. And then, because they were old friends, he admitted that he was about as essential to the operation as a rubber crutch.

"As long as they're paying you, don't knock it," Terry said.

131

They had dinner together, and before they parted, Tony was invited to come to the pit early in the morning "and see how the poor people live."

Tony's reply was that he would, "if I can find the time."

He went in the morning to the Firebrand garage area and found that he was no more needed in the morning than he had been the day before. He hung around for half an hour, and saw that not only was he not needed, but actually in the way.

He headed for the pit area, where his red badge gained him entrance without question. He found Terry and Terry's car. It wasn't very impressive. It was an eight-year-old Chevrolet which had been altered and modified so as to be just barely recognizable. It had a big vane mounted on angle irons above it.

"That's what you call a spoiler," Terry said. "In theory, it holds the car onto the ground, an upside-down wing. Sometimes I have an almost uncontrollable urge to tell the tower I'm rolling, to pull back on the wheel and soar off into the wild blue yonder."

"I used to drive sports cars," Tony said. "But I don't know very much about these."

"If I don't bang it up in the race," Terry said, "I'll let you take a lap or two. It may not be the greatest thrill in the world, and it's certainly one of the world's less comfortable means of transportation, but it would be, I think, an experience for you."

"You'd trust me with it?" Tony asked.

"It's not all that difficult," Terry said. "You're not going to race with it. And you used to be a fair-to-middling

132

chopper driver. I think you could get it around the track a couple of times without wrapping it up." He smiled, and then went on, "But then, maybe I sort of subconsciously hope you do tear it up. That would make me get out of modifieds and into Grand National."

"Is that what you want to do?" Tony asked. "Get into Grand National Racing?"

"That's what we all want to do," Terry said. "Everybody in this business wants in Grand National."

"Why don't you, then?" Tony asked.

"I will," Terry said. "I will. Eventually. But if you're asking why not now?"

"OK, why not now?"

"When I took off Uncle's suit, I took a solemn vow that I had been in my last organization," Terry said. "Or, at least, an organization where I wasn't the big cheese. That eliminates one way into Grand National, which is driving on somebody's team—the Firebrand Team, for example. When I go into Grand National, I'll be on my own."

"What keeps you from doing that?"

Terry rubbed his thumb and index finger together in the universal gesture meaning money. "There are two ways to get a Grand National car," he said, "and the stuff that you have to have to go with it. One is to be born rich, and go buy one. Another is to have a good enough reputation so that you can borrow the money. I've got the reputation, but when you borrow money that way, it comes tied to a whole lot of conditions. You have to ask permission to breathe. The final way is to accumulate some dough, and have it ready when someone in Grand

133

National with his own equipment decides he wants out, either because he's had enough, or because he gets hired to drive on a team, or a guy with money comes along and buys in by hiring a driver and buying a car."

"Fascinating," Tony said.

"In the meantime, I race this old wreck, and save my money. I've almost got enough now," Terry said. "I think I just might have a little more two hours from now, too, unless the wheels fall off."

"Good luck," Tony said.

"You don't happen to have, Lieutenant, sir, a small amount of loot, say five or ten thousand, that you'd be willing to put on your ol' buddy, do you?"

"Sure," Tony said. "I carry it around in my shirt pocket as petty cash."

Terry laughed. He didn't expect Tony to have any money, of course. But the odd thing was that Tony did have a large amount of cash, almost nine thousand dollars. He hadn't deliberately saved it, on any sort of a savings plan. It was simply a matter of having earned, in the army in Vietnam, a good deal more money than he could spend—and his tastes had been simple there. He'd drawn a hundred and fifty dollars a month for pocket money, and the difference, more than five hundred dollars, had gone directly to his bank each month, to join the three thousand already there before he went to Vietnam.

He would, as soon as he got his feet on the ground and had time to consider the matter, invest it somewhere. But at the moment, Terry had hit very close to home. Tony did have a large amount of cash.

The modified race began at 11:00 o'clock. Tony realized that his Press badge would permit him to watch the race from the Press Box, but he decided that that would be slightly dishonest, since he wasn't really part of the working press, so he found himself an open spot in the infield, and watched the race from there.

By the fifteenth lap, it was apparent to him that Terry was a first class driver; that, in other words, Terry was really driving very well, and that the enthusiasm Tony felt was not based entirely on the fact that they had often flown together. But he thought of this, and remembered that Terry, unlike himself, had been one of those "natural" pilots, a man born with superior reflexes, whose mind gave him extraordinary physical skill. He had been a superb pilot, and it was evident that he was just about as good a race driver.

Tony thought, of course, of Terry and the Firebrand racing team. It would be nice if Terry were driving a Firebrand. At least he'd have someone to talk to. But that seemed to be out of the question, a wide area of wishful thinking. If Terry was as good as he looked, he would have had the offer before this. Perhaps he had had it, and turned it down. Tony remembered what Terry had said about wanting nothing to do with an organization.

It was just possible, Tony thought, that Terry could make it on his own. He hoped his old friend could.

Tony had enough experience as a sports car racing driver to make a professional guess as to Terry's track strategy. It had become immediately apparent that the car Terry was driving had a great deal of power, a tre-

135

mendous acceleration. But Terry was running fourth and fifth and even sixth, instead of out front. Tony thought that he was doing this because it was safe. There was severe competition for first place, and the lap money that came with it. Staying back where he was, Terry was spared the competition, and the risk of being smashed into and out of the race.

The modified race was for 100 laps. Terry had never moved closer to leading the race than fourth position until the 90th lap. In the 91st lap, with two of the original forerunners already out of the race, and as if to prove that Tony's guess had been right, Terry began to move up.

Tony detected a slight increase in speed as Terry's old Chevy came down the start/finish straightaway, and he thought that Terry had taken an extra fraction of a second before lifting his foot from the accelerator to slow for the first turn.

He lost sight of Terry after Terry entered the first turn, and couldn't see him again, because of where he was standing, until Terry had rounded the second turn and was coming back onto the straight section of track before the stands.

He was now in third position, outside, and there was a suggestion of a fishtail as he accelerated coming out. He was moving very fast, right next to the barrier between the track and the stands, and he moved past the car in second position just about the time it was necessary to slow for the first turn again. He dropped back in third going into the turn, and he was still in third spot when

Tony could see him next, coming on the start/finish straightaway again.

This time, he moved, still outside, past the car in second position before they were halfway down the straightaway, in time for him to pull in ahead of the car he'd just passed.

The car in the lead position was moving faster now, with Terry two car lengths behind him, and running no more than ten yards ahead of the car in third. On the next lap, the car in third position made a valiant attempt to get past Terry, and with a sick feeling, Tony saw that he was going to succeed.

Apparently flushed with that victory, the driver who had been in third position and was now in second, stayed outside, held his foot to the floor, and moved into the lead. Both cars picked up ten, then twenty, then thirty yards on Terry, as they competed for the first spot. The rest of the pack was fifty yards and more behind the three cars out in front.

On the 98th lap, the car which had lost first place regained it, and Terry closed the distance between him and the two cars ahead of him. On the 99th lap Terry went outside, and then apparently ran the Chevy just as fast as it would go for as long as he dared before slowing for the first turn. He managed to pull parallel, and then ahead of the car in second place, and to put his front fender beside the rear fender of the front runner, but it wasn't enough to change his relative position; he dropped back into third place as he entered the turn.

On the last lap, he tried again, and Tony's heart fell as he saw that Terry wasn't going to make it on the straight-

137

away. The only chance Terry had was to try a final time on the back stretch, and Tony wouldn't be able to see that. Impatiently, he waited for the cars to reappear coming onto the final stretch of road before the checkered flag would signal the end of the race.

Coming out of the second turn, Terry Boag's battered old Chevrolet was in first place. But then the blue Ford, the car which had been in first place, and lost it, and then regained it, moved up, inside, going very very fast. It would be, Tony thought, even as it was happening, a test of acceleration now.

And the blue Ford had more power than Terry's Chevrolet. It inched up, drew parallel, and in the split second before the two cars crossed the line, moved ahead. Terry had come in second.

Tony thought, based on how he would have reacted in a situation like that, that Terry would be glum, annoyed that he hadn't been able to take, due to his car, the race his skill had just about earned him.

When he pulled into the pits, however, Terry was anything but glum. He was tired and showed it, but he was smiling.

"The good guys win again," he said, taking eagerly the Coke Tony handed him.

"Don't look now, but you came in second," Tony said.

"According to the Great Operations Plan," Terry said. "The Objective was placing. I would have been satisfied with fourth, which paid $1500. I would have been delighted with third, which paid $1750. I am overjoyed, ol'

138

buddy, with the $2500 second place earned. It puts me precisely one thousand clams closer to a decent car than I hoped I would be."

Terry's pit crew went over the car, fueled it, changed the left front tire and wheel, and prepared to roll it onto a flat-bed trailer-transporter. Tony and Terry had been sitting on the low concrete block wall separating their pit from the one beside it. Terry was obviously beat. It wasn't, Tony thought, a great deal different from the fatigue they'd often experienced after a mission. It was enough just to sit still, and a real luxury to have something cold to drink. He was not going to bring up Terry's offer of before the race to let him drive the car.

Terry suddenly remembered it.

"Hey, knock that off," he called to the pit crew. "The Mad Russian's going to take a couple of laps in it."

"Has he got a license?" one of the crewmen asked.

"Probably not," Terry said. "But I won't squeal if you won't."

"It's your car, Terry," the crewman said. "What are you going to say if someone asks?"

"I'll swear I never saw him before in my life," Terry said. "Come on, Russian Joe, I'll give you a quick pre-flight checkout."

He went to a wooden crate and came back with a set of coveralls. Tony slipped into them, and then Terry handed him a helmet.

"Very simple machine to operate," Terry said, when Tony was in the bucket seat and Terry was tightening the

139

seat belt. "That long, thin thing is the go pedal. The thing with the handle shifts gears, and you remember what clutch and brake pedals are for, don't you?"

"I think you do hope I wrap it up for you," Tony said.

"Like I said, Russian Joe," Terry said. "I'm a whole thousand clams closer to getting a Grand National car. But try not to bend it; explaining you to the track officials might be just a little tricky."

The instruments the car had come with had been stripped from behind the dashboard. They had been replaced with large black-and-white instrumentation, except for a speedometer. There was no speedometer. There was a toggle switch with ON written above it with a Magic Marker, and beneath it a chrome button, obviously the starter.

"Clear?" Tony asked, mocking the starting procedure for a helicopter. Terry went along with the gag.

"Clear," he repeated, and made a circling, wind-it-up motion with his index finger. Tony pushed the toggle switch to the ON position and then pushed the starter. There was a grinding sound, and then the engine, still warm, came back to life. When he tapped the accelerator, the torque moved the car from side to side against the springs. Tony looked at Terry Boag, and Terry gave him the aviator's signal, the index finger extending and pointing, for takeoff.

Tony put the car in gear, surprised at the amount of pressure required to push down on the clutch pedal. He tapped the accelerator again, and then let the clutch out. The wheels chirped, although he had made an effort to

140

move very slowly, and then the car was moving down the pit road. Tony moved the gearshift into second and stepped a little harder on the accelerator. The car responded immediately. There was a great deal of power.

When he turned onto the track itself, he put the shift lever in high and started to move more rapidly. He was surprised, even though he was used to the hard suspension of sports cars and trucks, how roughly this thing rode. He could feel every pebble and crack in the road.

He was moving now at what he thought was a good clip, but when he looked down at the large circular tachometer, the needle was a long distance from a piece of red plastic tape that obviously indicated maximum safe revolutions.

He turned the wheel to enter the first turn, and felt a slight tug of centrifugal force pushing him down against the none-too-ample cushion on the seat. Coming out of the first turn, he locked his wrists on the wheel and put his foot hard to the floor. The engine roared and the car picked up speed.

It was very noisy inside the car, a combination of engine roar, transmission whine and a steady thumping sound from the transmission. He had no idea how fast he was going, but there was still a good inch between the red tape on the tachometer and the tach needle.

In the second turn, he felt a greater push of centrifugal force, and it was necessary to apply more pressure to the steering wheel to move it. He liked the sure feeling of control, and the power available to him under the accelerator. He came out of the second turn as fast as he

141

dared, and held his foot to the floor as he went down the start/finish straightaway past the pits.

He had forgotten how much he missed driving a fast car. He hadn't, he realized, exceeded a speed limit in over three years. He realized that the polite thing to do now with Terry's car was to turn it into the pit after the second, or certainly after the third lap. What he wanted to do was keep driving this car for the rest of the afternoon. He took four laps, and then pulled into the pit.

"Well, Tony, what do you think?"

"If that car couldn't beat the Ford, that Ford must be quite a car."

"I thought you might enjoy this," Terry said. "But you ought to get behind the wheel of a Grand National. Now *there's* power."

Tony thought that since he had nothing else to do with the Firebrand team, he just might try to mooch a ride in a Firebrand. He could call it research, or something.

Terry Boag's crew loaded the car onto the trailer then, and he and Tony shook hands.

"If you're going to be around the tracks, Tony, I'll see you again." Terry said.

"I hope so," Tony replied, as Terry got into the front seat of a Chevrolet Carryall, and slammed the door.

11

When the race was over, a Firebrand having had the good fortune to run first again, Tony was in the pit area and able to watch the motion picture crew efficiently get the final feet of film of the winning car and driver. As soon as filming was over, one of the assistant cameramen took the film from that camera, as well as the film previously shot, loaded it into one of the cars the team had rented, and left, obviously to get the film to New York.

The rest of the film crew filmed the Firebrand team as it packed up to leave Darlington for the Atlanta International Raceway in Georgia. It wasn't, Tony realized, that they were being impolite to him, but simply that he really had nothing to do.

He drove back to his motel and called Skeezix James at his home.

"Something wrong, Tony?" Skeezix asked, and there was suspicion in his voice.

"No. Everything went smoothly," Tony said. "Fire-

143

brand won, they got good film, which is on the way to New York, and the crew is on its way to Atlanta. I'm just calling for orders, so to speak. What would you like me to do now?"

"Catch a plane back up here, why don't you? It might be useful if you were here at noon tomorrow when we show the rough-cut film."

"I'll be there," Tony said. "Sorry to bother you at home."

"No bother, Tony," Skeezix said. "That's what you're supposed to do, and what I'm here for."

The first plane that he could catch put him into New York at 10:40 the next morning. He got to the office just before noon, and Mrs. Berkowitz told him that the showing of the film had been delayed, and rescheduled for two in the afternoon.

Tony picked Barbara up at her office, and they went to a small restaurant and had lunch.

At five minutes to two, Tony went to Skeezix' office. Mr. Crosby from the Detroit office was there, and so, surprisingly, was Mr. Garrett. Crosby seemed something less than overjoyed to see Tony, but Skeezix greeted Tony warmly.

The film was shown. This time there were two commercials, one running 90 seconds, and one running 60 seconds. Both looked better than the one Tony had supervised. There was also a tape recording, with sound effects, a make-believe radio broadcast of the last seconds of the race, with, of course, the name *Firebrand* mentioned very frequently.

144

Garrett was obviously pleased.

"You write those, Fletcher?" he asked.

"No, sir— Tony began, and Crosby smoothly cut him off.

"Actually, they were written both at the track and in my shop by my people," he said.

"Tony's monitoring the whole operation," James said quickly. He got looks of surprise from both Tony and Mr. Crosby; the implication was that Tony had had more to do, and Crosby less, with the operation than was actually the case.

"Well, whatever you're doing, Fletcher, keep it up," Garrett said.

"Yes, sir," Tony said. (I will do twice as much as I have been doing, and the net result will be nothing because two times nothing is still nothing.)

"Have you had a chance to drive a Firebrand?" Garrett asked.

"I rented a Seneca stationwagon," Tony said. "They didn't have a Firebrand for hire."

"I believe in experience," Garrett said. "You take a couple of laps in a racing Firebrand."

"Yes, sir."

"We're on the right track now, gentlemen," Garrett said, and got up and walked out of the room with only a nod of his head for a good-bye. When he was sure that Garrett was out of hearing, Skeezix said:

"You know, it doesn't really matter who does the work, so long as Garrett likes it, and the firm pleases him."

Tony wasn't sure if the remark was directed to him, or

145

to Crosby. After a moment, he realized that James had been talking to both of them.

"What are your plans now, Tony?" James went on.

"Well, the next race is Saturday, at Atlanta. I'm going down there, of course."

"Go down there on Wednesday," James said. "Stick around here a day or two, and do some more thinking."

Tony spent Monday afternoon in his office, first making out his expense account, and then because he had nothing else to do, looking at the film the team had shot and which had not been used.

When Barbara Chedister came out of her office, she found Tony waiting for her. Because it seemed like a good idea, and the day was so pleasant, they walked all the way uptown from the office to her apartment. He was introduced to her landlady, who didn't seem overly impressed with him, and afterward, they went up to the Golden Samovar for an early supper. Leo Orlovsky was even worse than Barbara. So far as he was concerned, having a job like Tony's, actually being paid to go to the car races all over the country, was a dream job. They made Tony feel as if he were some sort of chronic malcontent for not being able to see this.

Tuesday Tony spent all day first researching race information, and then writing what he thought would be good copy for the commercials that would come out of the Atlanta Races the next weekend. About four o'clock, he went to Skeezix James's office and waited forty-five minutes until Skeezix was free to see him.

James wouldn't even look at what Tony had written.

146

"We're getting involved here in areas of responsibility, Tony," Skeezix said. "If I sent your copy out to Crosby— or even if I looked at it—he would very likely take offense. Firebrand copy is his responsibility."

"I'm just trying to earn my keep," Tony said.

"The boss decides whether or not you're earning your keep," James said. "I'll let you know when I'm dissatisfied."

Tony and Barbara went to the movies that night, and Tony was on an early morning jet to Atlanta. Avis rental cars had a Seneca Firebrand for hire. Tony had to wait at the airport until one could be delivered from the garage in the city, and then he drove out to the Speedway. The Administration Office had never heard of Tony Fletcher, but they had a direct teletype connection with NASCAR headquarters at Daytona, and were willing to send a telegram to ask about him.

They were so pleasant to him that, while he was waiting for a reply from Daytona, Tony asked how one went about getting a NASCAR racing license. He found out that his Sports Car Club of America license, which was still valid, was good enough to get him a NASCAR apprentice license. Before he would be allowed to race, he would have to pass a road test given by NASCAR officials, and compete in a novice race.

By the time the Telex machine chattered out the information that Tony was to be given press credentials, he had filled out the forms and been issued a temporary novice license.

He found the Firebrand team and looked up its chief.

Doubt and unwillingness were written all over the team chief's face when Tony brought up the subject of driving a Firebrand.

"I don't know, Fletcher," he said. "I got the word from Detroit that we were to make ourselves as accommodating to you as possible, but nothing was said about you driving a car."

"It wasn't my idea," Tony said reluctantly.

"I'm afraid I'd have to get clearance from Detroit before I could let you drive one," the team chief said.

"Mr. Garrett *told* me to drive one," Tony said. "I won't bang it up, and I know how you feel."

"You'd have to get a license," the team chief said, and Tony was glad that he took his word for Garrett's having told him to drive one. "I wonder if Garrett thought about that?"

"I have a novice license," Tony said.

"You do?" the team chief asked. He was obviously surprised. "How'd you manage that?"

"I've got a valid SCCA license," Tony said.

"Well, that's all you need," the team chief said. "You don't happen to have a helmet and a racing suit, do you?"

"No, I don't."

"We can fix you up, I guess," the team chief said. "Come on."

"Now? Before the race?"

"There is one ironclad rule on the Firebrand racing team," the team chief said. "Very simple. Don't argue with Garrett."

"I've sort of felt that myself," Tony said, with a smile. The team chief smiled back at him.

148

"Who's to say he's wrong?" the team chief said. "I don't happen to be a vice-president."

Tony was given a fire-resistant racing suit and a racing helmet from the parts truck, and the team chief walked with him to the pits, where four Firebrands sat. Three would be entered in the race; the fourth was a backup.

The drivers, who recognized Tony from Daytona and Darlington, stared at him now with curiosity. He was the last person they expected to see in a racing suit.

"You all remember Mr. Fletcher from the advertising agency?" the team chief said, and various signs of acknowledgment of this, none very cordial, were made.

"Mr. Fletcher has a valid Sports Car license," the team chief said. "And he has a NASCAR novice license. But that isn't why he's going to take a couple of laps in one of the cars."

"How come then?"

"Because Mr. Garrett told him to take a ride in one of our cars," the team chief said. "*That's* how come."

There were smiles, and then, in unison, two drivers said, "And nobody argues with Garrett, right?"

"Right," the team chief said.

"Come on, Mr. Fletcher," one of the drivers said, motioning Tony toward one of the cars. He opened the door for Tony and Tony got behind the wheel.

"You ever drive on a track before?"

"Just once," Tony said. "Terry Boag let me take a couple of laps in his modified at Darlington."

"Is that so?" the driver said. That information obviously carried a good deal more weight than Mr. Garrett's orders. "How long you known Terry?"

149

"We were in the army together," Tony said.

"Terry was a helicopter pilot, is that what you were?"

"Uh huh."

"Well, then, maybe you won't bend it up," the driver said. "Let's see how the pedals fit." He bent down and then adjusted the track of the bucket seat so that Tony's feet were the correct distance from the foot pedals.

"That ought to do it," the driver said. "Can I ask you something?"

"Sure."

"Why does Garrett want you to drive one of these?"

"For experience, I guess," Tony said, and then he clarified this. "So I'll know what I'm writing about."

"I thought that little character with the funny-looking sports coat was writing these commercials."

"He is," Tony said.

"But Garrett thinks you are?"

"Something like that."

"And yours not to reason why?"

"Right."

"I had a lot of experience myself in the 'mine not to reason why' department," the driver said. "I was in the army, too." When Tony had laughed with him, he went on, "These are very well sprung, and they handle well. I wouldn't try to see how fast it will go, if I were you, but you can take it up to about here," he pointed at a blue mark on the tachometer. "That's 135 mph, or thereabouts. The green mark is about 145, and the red is 150. It'll go faster, but I don't think *I'd* want to tell Garrett *I'd* torn up one of his cars."

150

"I have always believed that cowardice has its place," Tony said.

"The starter's hooked to the ON position on the ignition toggle switch," the driver said. "Wind it up."

Tony pressed the toggle switch upwards, and the Firebrand shook as the starter engaged. The engine caught immediately, and then died as Tony flooded it by stepping on the accelerator too soon. He ground the starter again, and finally, with a cloud of bluish white smoke coming out the exhaust, the engine started again.

It idled roughly. Tony knew what caused this. In a physics classroom, teachers had solemnly discussed a particular metal's coefficient of linear expansion. It was fairly evident here: An engine whose parts would fit closely when that engine was running at high speed, and with the high temperatures high speed produced, would have to be loose when the engine was cold. Otherwise, when it was hot, it would be literally too tight to run when heat expanded its parts.

Tony sat there and let the engine idle until the water temperature and oil temperature gauges began to move. Then he put the shifter into low, released the clutch, and felt the awesome power of the engine pass through the transmission to the wheels.

He went up into second before getting out of the pit area, and into third almost as soon as he was on the track itself. He pressed down on the accelerator, deciding that he would need about 65 or 70 miles per hour to get around the banked turns. Since there was no speedometer, he estimated that if the blue mark on the tachometer

151

indicated 135 miles an hour, then a point halfway between 0 revs and the blue mark would be about half that fast, or 65–70 miles an hour.

The car moved through the first turn with ease. He dropped his eyes to the gauges, and saw that the temperature indicators were still a little shy of being in the green-marked safe operating zones. He went down the backstretch at the same speed he'd made going through the first turn, and then he went through the second turn. Coming out of it, the gauges told him that he was at a normal operating temperature. He pressed hard on the accelerator. He anticipated a reaction more than a simple increase in speed—the power of the engine was obvious —but not what he got: Despite the 70 miles per hour he was making, despite all the rubber on the track that the big racing tires provided, the wheels spun and the Firebrand fishtailed.

He quickly compensated for it, but he was startled none the less. He nursed the car faster, and the acceleration was tremendous. When he released the pressure of his foot on the accelerator to enter the first turn, the needle of the tach wasn't far from the blue mark indicating 135 mph.

In the turn, he felt the pressure of centrifugal force. It was far more severe than he'd felt driving Terry Boag's modified. It was closer to the G (for Gravity) pressures he'd known as a pilot. The ride was rougher, too. He could feel the uneven places, and the cracks in the pavement. As he came out of the turn, he decided that he would try to get pretty close to 135 mph going down the straightaway past the pits. He increased the pressure of his foot on the accelerator, and held it down as he heard the engine's roar increase in pitch.

The track was four lanes wide here, but from inside the car, it seemed to be sort of a funnel. The second turn came up very quickly and he was into it far faster than he had had any intention of going. He felt a double pressure now, the same force he'd felt before pressing him against the seat, and another, lesser pressure, trying to force him outward and upward. The car handled well. Just past the halfway point of the turn, in the fraction of a second before he pressed on the accelerator to accelerate out of the turn, he dropped his eyes to the tach. The needle was past the blue mark at 135, past the green mark at 145 and touching the red mark which signified 150 mph. Since he had slowed to enter the turn, it was obvious that he'd run over 150 on the straightaway.

It was at once thrilling and chilling. He had no right to be driving that fast.

But he hadn't, he realized, had any feeling that he was losing control, that the car was getting ahead of him. He decided he would try it again, making an effort this time to go no faster than 135 or 140. There were other cars on the track now, and he realized with chagrin that he hadn't been checking his rear view mirror nearly often enough.

There was no one behind him when he looked now, and he estimated tht he could get around the two cars directly ahead of him with no effort before reaching the first turn.

153

He pushed down on the accelerator. He had either underestimated the speed of the two cars on the track ahead of him, or, he thought, more likely, they had speeded up themselves. He wasn't going to be able to pass them with ease; there was now a question in his mind that he would be able to pass them at all before reaching the first turn.

Aware only of his control of the car, and not paying any attention to the tachometer, or the marks on it, Tony pressed harder on the accelerator. He got around the red Ford without any effort, but the yellow Ford ahead of it was going still faster. He was into the turn, and Tony was right on his tail, when for the first time he sensed that he was driving right on the edge of too fast.

Too fast, on a highway, suggests being over the speed limit, going too fast for absolute safety. Too fast on a race track, at these speeds, meant that he was right on the edge of losing control.

There was nothing to do now but continue applying pressure on the gas pedal and thus torque, to the wheels. It would be disastrous to try to slow entering a turn. He entered the turn right on the tail of the yellow Ford. He allowed himself to slip sideways and to the top of the banked turn as they passed through it. He felt a sudden cold chill as the barrier at the top of the turn appeared in the corner of his eye. The instant he could, he shoved his foot harder to the floor. The response was not immediate, and he felt a foul taste in his mouth as his mind painted a detailed picture of himself striking the guard rail and going out of control.

154

When he was no more than two feet from the guard rail, the tremendous torque of the engine overcame centrifugal force. The Firebrand straightened out, and Tony came out of the turn high, fast and outside. He went past the yellow Ford before he had gone two hundred yards down the rear stretch, and the Ford receded in his rear view mirror.

He dropped his eyes to the tachometer. The needle was three-quarters of an inch beyond the red mark that indicated 150 miles per hour. He gently eased off on the accelerator. If he had simply removed his foot at that speed, he very possibly would have lost the generator belt, or caused more damage to the engine.

He kept slowing as he entered the second turn, accelerated just a little coming out of it, to maintain control, and then slowed again, finally braking to enter the pit access road. He became aware then that he was sweat soaked, and that the muscles on his right leg were vibrating of their own accord.

He pulled into the pits, and was embarrassed when he stepped too hard on the brakes and skidded before stopping. He reached up and pulled the ignition switch toggle down. The engine coughed once and died, and suddenly it was very quiet in the car, with nothing but the *ping* of cooling engine parts. For half a second, Tony wondered if he was about to get sick to his stomach, but he forced that thought from his mind, opened the door, unfastened the seat belt and got out.

He noticed then, for the first time, that a camera crew

was in place, and that the cameras were pointing at him. He took off the helmet, and then he heard a voice call in disgust.

"Cut! That's Fletcher!"

Somebody laughed, and then there was a general sound of laughter, coming from the drivers and the pit crews, and obviously directed at the camera crew and the copywriter from Mr. Crosby's office in Detroit. He came charging over to Tony, and just as Tony decided that the driver was right, he did wear funny-looking sports coats, the copywriter demanded:

"Would you mind telling me what you're doing driving one of those?"

"I will, if you'll tell me why you're taking my picture," Tony replied.

The copywriter flushed angrily. "They told me," he said, gesturing in the general direction of the pit crew, "that something interesting was liable to happen to this car."

"I guess maybe they thought I'd wreck it," Tony said.

"What were you doing driving it?" he demanded.

"I was told to drive it," Tony said. "OK?"

"I'm going to have to tell Crosby, you understand," the copywriter said.

"Go ahead," Tony said. "Tell him anything you want to tell him." He was tired and sweat soaked, and, added to this, he had an inspiration. It would make a good commercial, he had suddenly realized, if there were a camera set up in what had been, before the seats were removed, the back seat. The camera would point down the track,

156

while an official-sounding voice counted off the speed. One Fifty. One fifty-one. One fifty-five.

Tony decided that as soon as he had a shower, he'd find a typewriter somewhere and send the idea, as Skeezix had made it quite clear he should, to Crosby. It was such a good idea that even Crosby couldn't shoot it down.

By the time he'd gone back to the motel and taken a shower, his enthusiasm had dimmed to the point that he thought he'd better check with Skeezix. He reached for the telephone when he was still dripping wet from the shower.

"What's on your mind, Tony?" Skeezix said. He seemed something less than overjoyed to hear Tony's voice.

"I just drove a Firebrand—a racing machine. As per instructions," Tony said.

"And?"

"I sort of had the feeling that Mr. Garrett thought that I might be inspired."

"I gather you weren't?"

"Sort of. I've got an idea for a commercial—a camera inside the car as it goes around the track. If you think it's worth while, I'll spend the rest of the day writing it up and sending it to Mr. Crosby for his—for whatever he wants to do with it."

"Sounds good to me," James said. "Write it up and send me a carbon."

"Yes, sir," Tony said. "That's all I had, thank you."

12

Finding a typewriter proved something of a problem. After calling three typewriter rental agencies without being able to have one promised immediately, Tony drove from the motel into Atlanta proper and bought a portable at Rich's Department Store.

Then he drove back to the motel, wrote several drafts, and finally, very neatly typed a final version with two carbons, and then a very polite, humble letter to Mr. Crosby, offering the idea for his consideration. Then he drove over to the Airport Branch of the Post Office and mailed the original to Mr. Crosby, and the carbon to Skeezix James, Air Mail Special Delivery. Both would have it in their hands first thing the next morning.

With the work out of the way, he suddenly remembered that he hadn't had any lunch. He had, he thought, for the first time in a long time, done enough work to justify feeding himself a steak. He looked for a restaurant on the way back to his motel, and when he saw a large red neon sign reading simply: STEAKS, he pulled into its parking lot.

It was a pleasant-appearing restaurant, filled with the pleasant odor of broiling meat, and he began to scan the menu as soon as he was shown to a small table.

"What's the matter, Barney Oldfield?" a voice said in his ear. "Have you been banished from the publicity crew?"

He looked up and saw one of the drivers. Behind him, three other drivers and three young women were sitting at a table.

"I don't use Brisk, I guess," Tony said.

"Come on over and join us," the driver said. "I guess we're responsible."

"I'd like that," Tony said, meaning it. It would be nice for a change to have someone to talk to, over dinner.

He was introduced to the girls as "one of the advertising guys," and it was apparent that to the girls "one of the advertising guys" didn't have nearly so much appeal as any of the drivers.

"You had your neck out pretty far today, Fletcher," one of the drivers said, "but I have to admit, you looked pretty good out there."

"Those are amazing cars," Tony said. "I've never driven anything like that before."

"Somebody said you used to race sports cars?"

"There's no comparison," Tony said. "None whatever."

"You did pretty good," another driver said.

"I used to be a truck driver," Tony said. "Maybe that helped."

"You used to drive a truck? Panel? Delivery? What?"

159

"I used to drive a cross-country rig," Tony said and, smiling, produced both his chauffeur's license and his Teamster's Union membership card.

"So did I," the driver who had seemed to doubt his word said, and produced his Teamster's card. "Excuse me, but you don't look like the type."

"I look like an advertising type, is that what you mean?" Tony asked.

"Not dressed the way you are now," the driver said, "but the way you're normally dressed at the track."

"I used to wear a uniform in the army, too," Tony said.

"He was in the army with Terry Boag," the driver who had helped Tony into the car earlier said.

"You know Terry, do you?" the first driver said. Tony nodded, and that, added to the Teamster's Union card, seemed to lower the last barrier between them. He stopped being some jerk visitor and became another individual, with a first name. It was a far more pleasant supper than he had anticipated, and when he got back to the motel, he called Barbara to tell her what a good day he had had.

A Dodge Charger came from behind and took the Atlanta 500 away from the Firebrand Team, but Tony wasn't especially depressed. They couldn't expect to win every time. He thought, he hoped objectively, that the loss had been a fluke; that the Firebrands, and their drivers, were really the best, and could expect to win a substantial portion of the races in which they were entered.

The day of the race, there had been an early morning telephone call from Mrs. Berkowitz. The film of that

160

week's racing would be shown to Mr. Garrett in Detroit. Tony was to go there, rather than to New York.

Tony followed what he thought was the proper protocol. He called Mr. Crosby when he arrived in Detroit. He did not mention the copy he'd sent to him, and Crosby didn't bring it up. Tony offered to meet Crosby at the Detroit offices of Collier, Richards & Company, and was told, instead, to meet "everyone" at Garrett's office in the Amalgamated Motors Building. Crosby obviously wanted it crystal clear, despite the little speech he'd been given by Skeezix James, that A. Fletcher, Esq. was not part of the Crosby team.

Garrett had little to say about the new television and radio commercials, and simply nodded at the printed advertisements that had been prepared over the past week. Tony had seen none of them before, and they were, he thought, good.

And then his enthusiasm for his own ideas ran away with him again.

"Am I permitted to make a suggestion?" he asked.

"You're being paid to do just that, aren't you?" Garrett asked.

"I don't know if it would come out in a still picture," Tony said. "But what about a shot from inside a car, during a race? We could even play it a little impolite, and take it from an unidentifiable car, showing the rear of a Firebrand on a track, with a line like 'This is all they got to see of a *Firebrand* during the such-and-such race.'"

"I like it," Garrett said simply. "Do it."

"Certainly," Crosby said. "I was going to propose some-

161

thing like that. The same idea came—simultaneously, apparently—from the man I have with the team."

"What happens to you now, Fletcher?" Garrett asked.

"I don't know what you mean, Mr. Garrett," Tony said.

"I'll spell it out. You ever been around the Seneca factory before?"

"No, sir."

"It takes about two full days for a complete tour—and that's a complete tour. You got two days free?"

"Yes, sir."

"OK. Come with me, and I'll set it up with our Visitors' Bureau," Garrett said. "That's OK with you, Crosby, isn't it?"

"I think it's a splendid idea, Mr. Garrett," Crosby said with a warm smile. "Part of the reason for Fletcher's assignment is to broaden his experience base."

"Is that so?"

"I'd like a word with him before he starts, before I leave, if that would be all right with you, Mr. Garrett?"

"Why not? When he's finished with you, Fletcher, have someone show you the Visitors' Bureau."

"Yes, sir," Tony said. "Thank you."

When Garrett had gone, Crosby got right to the point: "I thought it was understood between you, Mr. James and myself, Fletcher, that any proposals to the client were to be routed via me, for my approval."

"I'm sorry, Mr. Crosby," Tony said. "I got carried away."

"When I was starting out, Fletcher, I was given a good piece of advice, which I pass on to you. Engage brain before opening mouth."

"Yes, sir."

"Since you seem to rather ignore me, Fletcher, I tell you frankly that I'm going to bring this up to Mr. James. Perhaps he can convince you that we are both serious when we say we want all material submitted through me."

"What about the material I submitted to you?" Tony said. "What was your opinion of that?"

"Frankly, I didn't think much of it. But keep trying, Fletcher."

"I will," Tony said.

"I frankly don't like your attitude, Fletcher," Crosby said.

"Sorry about that," Tony said. "I'll try to reform."

"I consider that insubordinate."

"The last I heard, I still work for Skeezix," Tony said. "Since you're not my boss, I can hardly be insubordinate. I have enough trouble being civil."

He turned and walked out of the room into the marble corridors of the Amalgamated Motors Building.

He was sorry he'd talked back by the time he had found the Visitors' Bureau. He didn't think that Skeezix would be unduly upset when Crosby ran to him with the tale of Tony having proposed a printed media rough, but Skeezix would be angry at Tony for having taken on Crosby in a verbal duel. Right and wrong weren't the issues. Crosby was a senior company official, the account executive for a major client. Tony had had no right to talk to him like that, and he knew it.

They were waiting for him in the Visitors' Bureau.

"You're not what I expected, frankly, Mr. Fletcher," a

young man of Tony's age said when Tony identified himself.

"What did you expect?"

"Mr. Garrett said give you the grand tour, you were the brain behind the new advertising campaign. I thought you'd be sort of a glorified Mr. Crosby."

"No such luck," Tony said. "I'm just one of the hired hands."

"Well, you're stuck with me for two days," the young man said. "I'm Paul Maradik." He put out his hand. Tony shook it. "The way I like to start is to show you a layout of the plant over a cup of coffee. Before we actually go out to see it."

"You're a man after my own heart," Tony said.

It was ten o'clock before Tony got back to his hotel. Not only had he walked, literally miles, through the Seneca plant, but Maradik, bringing his wife along, had taken him to dinner. They were a pleasant young couple, and Tony had enjoyed himself. He was in a good mood, until he reached his room, found the red light flashing on his telephone, and picked it up to learn that he was to call Mr. James at whatever hour he got in.

"I hope you had a good time tonight, loudmouth," James greeted him.

"The guy at the Seneca plant took me to dinner," Tony said. "I just got in."

"What guy at the Seneca plant?"

"Fellow named Maradik. Garrett set up a two-day tour of the plant for me, and Maradik lost the raffle and got stuck with me. He's a very nice guy."

164

"What exactly did you say to Garrett at the meeting that has Crosby's feathers so ruffled?"

"I proposed an idea without clearing it first with Crosby."

"And then you ran off at the mouth at Crosby, I gather?"

"He leans all over me," Tony said. "But I am sorry I let him have the lip."

"Look, stupid," James said. "You don't mind if I call you stupid, do you? I mean, after you keep proving it all the time?"

"I said I was sorry."

"Look, Tony," Skeezix said reasonably. "Crosby is an important man in the firm. He's going to be a vice-president sooner or later. In your own interests, stop waving a red flag in his face. He's the sort of guy who carries a grudge, and I won't always be here to protect you."

"I'm sorry," Tony repeated. "In the future, I'll keep my yap shut."

"For your own sake, I hope you can," Skeezix said. The phone went dead.

The next night, Tony took Mr. and Mrs. Maradik to dinner, and decided to pay for it himself, rather than putting it on the expense account. Maradik had really gone out of his way to give Tony a thorough tour of the Seneca plant, and Tony was grateful. He left Detroit early the next morning for Briston, Tennessee, where the Firebrand team would race the next weekend.

From the airport, he called all the motels until he found the one where the Firebrand team was staying.

165

They had a room for him. He hoped that it wouldn't look as if he had invited himself to a party.

They seemed glad to see him, and when he went to the track, he wore a sports shirt and slacks, rather than his "advertising suit." He was relieved and pleased that they accepted him in the pits, and had dropped the "Mister" from the "Mister Fletcher."

When it came time to leave the track at dusk, two of the drivers asked if he had room for them in his car, and when they got to the motel, they asked Tony to join them for a beer.

"Let's take a quick dip in the pool, and then find someplace to eat," one of the drivers said. "Unless you've got some other plans, Tony?"

"Sounds good to me," Tony said.

While they were in the pool, a stocky young man with unruly hair walked to the edge of it and shouted, "If you bums are all they have for drivers, no wonder they hired me."

The others climbed out of the pool and greeted the newcomer like a long lost brother. Then Tony was introduced.

"This is the guy that'll put you on TV," one of the drivers said. "Tony Fletcher, Red Clark."

"How are you, Fletcher?" Clark said.

"Red was an independent who finally came to his senses," the driver said.

"You don't know anybody who wants to buy a nearly new Dodge Charger, do you, Fletcher?"

"I don't know," Tony said. "Have you asked Terry Boag?"

Clark's face lit up. "No. But that's a good idea. Do you think he's got the dough?"

"We can call him and find out," Tony said.

"Not until I get some clothes on," the driver said. "He's racing at Charlotte, I think."

"What do you want for it?" Tony asked, as he dried himself.

"I'm asking twenty-five big ones for the package," Clark said. "I'll take twenty thousand in cash. But if I call Terry, I'm putting myself at a disadvantage."

"What if I call him, and act as sort of a go-between?" Tony asked.

"I'd appreciate it, Fletcher," Clark said.

Tony put in a person-to-person call from his room. He found out where Terry was staying, but there was no answer. Tony left word for him to call when he got in, and then they all went out to dinner.

The phone was ringing when Tony returned to his room.

"That's a buy at twenty," Terry said. "I'd need another five for operating expenses. Do you think he'd take fifteen thousand now, and five if and when I made it? If I promised him whatever I got for the Modified? If and when I sell that?"

"He wants twenty-five thousand, on terms," Tony said. And then the words were out of his mouth before he really considered what he was saying. "I'll loan you five thousand, if you want, Terry. For a piece of it."

There was a pause. "I won't ask if you can afford it," Terry said. "I already know that."

"What do you mean by that?"

"Tom Agostini reads *The New York Times*," Terry said. "He sent me that clipping about you. Where it said who your father is and all."

"This isn't my father's money," Tony said. "This is what I saved when I was in Vietnam."

"How much of a piece would you want?" Terry asked. "What would be fair?"

"You want to just loan me the money, or do you want to keep a piece?"

"Let's call it an investment," Tony said.

"How about fifteen per cent?" Terry said. "Or, if this would be all right with you, I'll pay you back at the rate of 20% of my winnings until you get your money back, and you'd still get ten per cent after that."

"That sounds good to me," Tony said.

"Borrowing money to enter Grand National racing is a lot harder than you think," Terry said. "There's a good chance we lose the whole thing, you know."

"I know," Tony said.

"How soon could you let me have the money?"

"I could give Clark a check right now, if you'd like," Tony said.

"You don't want a contract?"

"I don't think we need one," Tony said.

"OK, sucker," Terry said. "Give him the dough if you want to. Before somebody else beats us to it."

"I'll do it right now," Tony said.

"Thanks, Tony," Terry said. "I appreciate it. I hope you don't regret it before it's over."

Tony went to Red Clark's room with the check. Clark

had already gone to bed, and greeted Tony sleepy-eyed at the door.

He looked at the check and his eyebrows went up.

"Down payment," Tony said. "Twenty thousand in cash."

"That's what I asked for," Red Clark said, "and I think it's a fair price."

"Then why are you so glum?"

"Well, I like Terry," Red said. "And I have just decided that racing as an independent is a good way to go broke quick. I'd be happier, in other words, if I didn't like Terry."

"Terry's a big boy," Tony said. "He knows what he's doing."

"Do you?" Clark asked. "Do you know how quickly this five grand of yours can vanish on the Grand National circuit?"

"Terry's very good," Tony said. "Maybe it'll *grow* quickly."

"I hope so," Red said, and he put out his hand to shake on the deal and make it final.

13

Tony didn't actually get to see Terry for three weeks. Red had left the Dodge in Atlanta and once he took possession of it, Terry was wise enough to practice with the car in races not part of the Grand National Circuit.

In those three weeks, the Firebrand team had won only once. At North Wilksơoro, they hadn't even placed. It was hard to base an advertising campaign on cars that didn't make it regularly to the winner's circle; it was just about the same thing as telling people they should buy the second best, or the third best.

It was possible, of course, to spread winning commercials over a two- or three-week period, and hope that the people watching them didn't keep up with actual races in the meantime.

Tony saw Mr. Garrett only once during the three weeks, and he didn't seem angry, or even surprised, that the Firebrand team was doing badly. Crosby, on the other hand, seemed to take it as a personal affront, and it

170

took a good bit of self-discipline on Tony's part to keep his mouth shut, as promised, when Crosby bitterly complained.

Terry Boag and his Dodge showed up at the Langley Field Speedway at Hampton, Virginia. It was the first time Tony had seen the car, and he liked what he saw.

"Do you want to take it around the track for a couple of laps, partner?" Terry asked.

"No, thanks," Tony said. "I'd love to, but since it's the only one we have, let's see if we can't keep it in one piece."

"You could take a couple of slow laps," Terry said.

"Get thee behind me, Satan," Tony said. "Stop tempting me. I have very little moral fiber."

Terry laughed, but Tony saw that he was relieved he hadn't taken up the offer.

Tony had no thought that Terry, as an independent, was going to prove to be much of a challenge to the Firebrand team. Terry would be, he thought, one of those racers who didn't really push their luck, one of those more or less satisfied to place consistently, to bring home smaller checks, but to bring them home regularly.

Terry had different ideas, and he went about demonstrating their application immediately. In the time trials for starting position, he ran the Dodge around for a lap speed of 78.921. The track record, set by Dick Petty, was 80.801. Terry earned the second place spot on the starting grid. A Firebrand took the pole position.

When the flag went down, the Firebrand moved into the lead, but Terry was on his heels, and he stayed there.

171

For the first time, Tony had opportunity to consider the conflict of interest his investment in Terry's car represented. Personally, he was rooting for Terry, not only because of his money in the car, but because Terry was an independent racing against the organization; and Tony, like most people, was prone to root for the underdog.

In the 43rd lap, the Firebrand out in front blew a tire, and Terry moved around him into first place. The Firebrand which had been running fourth moved up to challenge him for the lead spot, but was unable to get around him until Terry had to go to the pits for fuel. Tony saw that Terry's pit crew was nowhere near as efficient as the Firebrand pit crew. Their relative inefficiency was going to cost Terry in the race.

Terry seemed well aware of this. When he came out of the pits, he really laid his foot heavy on the accelerator. In fifteen laps, he had made up, five and six seconds at a time, the extra 45 seconds he had lost in the pits.

The Firebrand carrying number 78, the third Firebrand entry, was still out in front as the end of the race drew near. Terry whipped past him, to lead the race for a lap and a half, but then Number 78 passed him again, and stayed out in front.

On the last lap, coming down the straightaway, Terry made a valiant effort to get out in front. He failed. The Firebrand had superior acceleration, and Number 78 went across the finish line fifteen yards before Terry's Dodge.

All things considered, Tony decided the race could not have ended any better. Terry had taken second place, and with it almost $5,000. After expenses, there would be probably close to $2,000 profit. The Firebrand had won, which would permit another week of "We Won" commercials, and perhaps even put a smile on Crosby's face.

The schedule this week called for Mr. Garrett to view the film in New York. Tony was in his office early the next day, with not much to do but kill time until the afternoon preview at one o'clock.

At eleven o'clock, he was summoned to Skeezix James's office. The projector was set up, and Mr. Crosby was there.

"Change of schedule?" Tony asked.

"No," Crosby said. "I wanted Mr. James to see this film before we show it to Mr. Garrett."

Tony had a premonition that he wasn't going to like what he was about to see, but, since he had had absolutely nothing to do with the filming, he couldn't understand how he could be blamed for anything.

The lights were dimmed and the film began to roll. It was a fairly standard version of what they had done before. The Firebrand was shown roaring around the track, and there was even the element of honesty involved with a few feet of the blown-tire Firebrand fighting for control before stopping. And then the final seconds of the race with Number 78 flashing across the finish line fifteen yards ahead of Terry's Dodge.

The lights went on.

"What do you think, Skeezix?" Crosby asked smoothly.

"Very nice," Skeezix said. "At least we won, for a change. That makes it easier to sell cars, doesn't it?"

173

"We just barely won, you noticed," Crosby said.

"Yeah, that Dodge just about stole the show."

"Did you have that same feeling, Mr. Fletcher?" Crosby asked. Tony had a sick feeling in the pit of his stomach.

"He almost won," Tony said.

"Would you like to tell Mr. James about your connection with that Dodge, Mr. Fletcher, or would you rather I did?"

"What's he talking about, Tony?" James asked.

"I own a piece of the Dodge," Tony said. "I suspect he's driving at a conflict of interest."

"That's what I'd call it, yes," Crosby said.

"What's this all about, Tony?" James asked.

"The guy that owns the Dodge is an old friend of mine. When the Dodge came up for sale—Red Clark, who used to own it, joined the Firebrand team—Terry Boag didn't have quite enough money to buy it, so I loaned it to him."

"Ouch," Skeezix said. "We'll have to tell Garrett, of course."

"That's going to be embarrassing, isn't it?" Crosby said. "For the firm, I mean. And particularly, since Mr. Garrett has shown such an interest in our bright young Mr. Fletcher."

"Tony," Skeezix said. "Why in the world—?"

"I think, Skeezix," Crosby said, "that what we've shown here is that it is a serious mistake to go off half-cocked at the whim of the client."

"What you mean," Tony said, "is that if I'd been working for you, this wouldn't have happened, because I never would have been working for you, right?"

"That's pretty good, Fletcher," Crosby said. "I couldn't have said it better myself."

Tony stood up.

"Where are you going?" Skeezix asked.

"I'm going to find a typewriter so I can type out my resignation," Tony said. "What else is there to do?"

"I'm sure," Crosby said, with unmistakable triumph in his voice, "that Mr. James will be happy to give you a fine recommendation."

Skeezix looked at both of them, but didn't say a word to either one.

Tony went to his office, put paper and carbon in Mrs. Berkowitz' typewriter, and then wrote out his letter of resignation. It was brief and to the point.

"It is obvious to me that, because of a gross and inexcusable lack of judgment on my part, I have placed the firm in an embarrassing position, which can only be partially rectified by this, the submission of my resignation, effective immediately."

He typed out two envelopes, one to Skeezix James, and the other addressed to Mr. Garrett in Detroit. He called for a messenger, had James's copy delivered, and the other sent to the mailroom, and then he went to the personnel office and showed Barbara the copy he'd kept for himself.

"Oh, Tony," she said. "How stupid of you!"

"Anthony S. for Stupid Fletcher," he said. "But let it be remembered, as his head sinks slowly under the waves,

175

that he was stupid, but not dishonest. It was a question of not thinking, not dishonesty."

"What are you going to do?"

"I'll probably wind up in the trucking business," Tony said. "I've begun to form the idea that I don't belong in advertising."

"That's absurd," she said. "You have a real feeling for it."

"Everybody's wrong but me, right? I wish I could agree with you, but I don't."

"You didn't tell me what you're going to do."

"Well, for a couple of weeks, at least, I'm going to watch my investment. Then, when the scab is healed, I think I'll go home." He paused. "Dragging my tail behind me."

"Then I won't see you any more?" she said, rather than asked.

"I can't imagine why you'd want to," he said. "But you'd be surprised how often we run trucks into New York."

"Don't be so much of a fool," she said. "I don't like you when you're feeling sorry for yourself."

"That makes two of us," he said. "I am my own candidate for Jerk of the Year."

By the time he got to Rockingham, North Carolina, to the North Carolina Motor Speedway, the news had preceded him. Since he was no longer connected with the Firebrand racing team, he had to buy a ticket to get inside. The ticket gave him access to the infield, but not the pits. He walked along the hurricane fence until he found

176

Terry's pit. He felt like a kid locked out of the play-ground.

"Well, well," Terry said when he saw him. "If it isn't General Fletcher of the Army of the Unemployed. What are you doing out there?"

"I figured you'd have some clever idea of how to get me inside," Tony said.

"As a matter of fact, that idea did flit through my mind," Terry said. He went to a tool box, lifted it up, and took a yellow tag out. He rolled it up so that it would fit through a hole in the fence.

It read: NORTH CAROLINA MOTOR SPEEDWAY. PIT AREA PASS. OWNER.

For some reason, it cheered Tony up. He felt less like a complete outsider, less like a parasite, than he had before. It was unquestionably true that he was a bona fide partial owner. He had a lot of money invested in Terry's Dodge.

When he'd passed through the pit area gate and gone back to the pit, Terry was waiting for him.

"As a matter of fact, I have been in the market for a strong back and a weak brain," he said. "If you happen to be looking for low-paid but honest employment, with hardly any future to speak of at all, you've found the right place."

"I used to be pretty good at washing cars," Tony said. "You have any cars that need washing?"

"I feel bad about this, Tony," Terry said, suddenly serious. "I'm awful sorry I cost you your job."

"When you get right down to it, I didn't have a job," Tony said. "So let's change the subject."

177

"OK, Tony," Terry said.

Several of the Firebrand drivers made a point of stopping by the pit. Tony managed to stop them before they offered condolences, because it really wasn't a funeral. He even stopped them from making nasty cracks about the guy with the funny-looking sports coat, who obviously was the man who had run to Crosby to tell him that Tony owned a piece of Terry Boag's Dodge.

With that subject out of the way, he and Terry turned their attention to the race at hand. It would be the fastest race Terry had yet run in Grand National racing. The track was only a mile, but it was fast. Cale Yarborough had set the track lap record, in a '68 Mercury, at 118.717 miles per hour. That meant each lap would take just over 30 seconds.

Terry seemed confident when he went out for the time trials, but his showing wasn't very good. His time of 115.060 put him far back on the starting grid. The three Firebrands entered each did better. One of them had taken the third place spot, and the other two were at seventh and ninth positions.

Once the race was on, Terry drove hard. He moved up quickly from the pack, and was running in sixth position, ahead of two of the three Firebrands entered, and behind a leading pack dominated by the Ford Motor Company: Four Fords and a Mercury.

The race was three hundred miles, on the one-mile track, three hundred laps, each just a few seconds over half a minute in length.

By the time he came in for fuel on the 110th lap, Terry

178

was in fifth place, having edged one of the Fords out. The pit crew's slow time cost him position, however, and it was the 180th lap before he could move back into fifth place. By then, a Firebrand, two Fords and a Plymouth were running ahead of him, and another Firebrand was in sixth place, right behind him.

Tony was allowing his mind to wander, to wonder what was really wrong with staying in racing. Terry was obviously a superb driver, and bound to be a success. Tony thought that he had enough experience to serve as a fairly well-qualified manager for an independent team. He knew something about engines, something about racing, and had some business experience. It just might be, he decided, what was in the cards for him.

On the 203rd lap, Terry tried to move ahead of the car in fourth place by staying outside of the first turn, and then accelerating down and across the track on the rear straightaway. He managed to get past the Plymouth immediately in front of him, but the Firebrand in third place was not about to give up his position. They ran fast into the turn. Terry put the Dodge into a drift. He was going too fast to get out of it. As if in slow motion, the Dodge moved closer and closer to the outside barrier, and then slammed broadside into it.

There was a terrible sound of tearing metal, as the thin metal of the fenders and side panels was torn away, and then something substantial, either the frame or the wheel itself hit something immovable on the barrier. The rear of the Dodge swung around, and then the front tore loose and the car spun across the track like a top. Its right side

179

hit, facing in the opposite direction from the race, a heavy concrete barrier pole. Then it stopped.

The caution flag went up, and the growl of a siren began. Tony ran as fast as he could down the access road. He was grabbed and stopped by two very large track policemen.

"That's my car, and my buddy's driving it!" he protested.

"You won't do him any good if you get run over," the policeman said, and after a moment, Tony realized that he was right, shook his head in agreement, and was turned loose.

The active imagination that had seen him a few moments before as the successful partner in a racing team now saw him at Terry Boag's funeral. He couldn't see where Terry had hit from where he was, but he was sure his worst suspicions were confirmed when he saw the ambulance returning up the track with all its red lights flashing and the siren screaming.

He peered into it as it passed, and was more than a little shocked to see Terry Boag sitting up in the front seat, beside the driver and the doctor. The ambulance slowed at the pit, the door opened, and Terry got out.

Tony ran back to the pit.

"Are you all right?" he asked.

"You know anybody wants to buy a sort of square Dodge?" Terry asked. "That's what we've got."

"What happened?" Tony asked, immensely relieved that Terry was all right.

Terry was all right to the degree he could make a

bad joke. "Well, I was doing all right when I had the lever in D for Drive," he said, with a perfectly straight face. "But when I put it in R for Race, it just came all apart."

"You're out of your mind, you know that?" Tony said, and wrapped his arms around him. "You're a certifiable nut."

"I'm broke," Terry said. "I know that."

"Let's get out of here," Tony said. "We can come back later and pick up the pieces."

"You know, a thing like that," Terry said, "could really scare a guy."

They went to the motel, and Terry took a long, hot shower. He came out of the bathroom with a towel around his waist to show Tony where he'd been bruised. "It's a good thing I hit my head first," he said. "That must have broken the force of the blow."

"Don't you want to go to a doctor?"

"Nope," Terry said, picking up fresh clothing and going back to the bath. "What I want is a shave, a cold beer, and a steak, in that precise order."

"You're sure?"

"Stop worrying, lieutenant, we're both out of the army."

"And out of a job."

"Let's talk about that tomorrow," Terry said. "Following my old ritual of never doing today anything unpleasant that can possibly be put off until tomorrow. By tomorrow, I might be dead."

It was intended as a joke, but it didn't come off that

181

way. Both of them were fully aware that some other drivers had not walked away from accidents like that.

Terry was dressed surprisingly quickly, and they walked across the motel parking lot to the restaurant.

By unspoken agreement, they did not discuss the race, or what would happen to the Terry Boag Racing Team now. They talked instead of the army and, of course, remembered only the funny things, not the horror. They were laughing out loud at something that had happened half a world away when a third man joined their table uninvited.

"I heard you had a bad sense of propriety," he said. "And I see you've got an odd sense of humor as well."

"Who's your peanut-sized pal, Tony?" Terry asked.

"He's got an odd sense of humor himself," Tony said. "He likes to go to wakes and gloat."

"Bring us three beers, young lady," the newcomer said.

"Mr. Boag, Mr. Garrett," Tony said.

"This little guy? This is the ogre himself? The way he scares people I thought he was nine feet tall and had fangs."

"Watch your lip, buddy," Garrett said. "Or I may have to reconsider my offer of employment."

That remark made Tony and Terry pay attention. The waitress delivered the three mugs of beer. Garrett picked his up. "Rest in peace, Faithful Dodge," he said. "You gave the corporate structure quite a scare for a while."

"I'll drink to that," Terry said. "That was a good car. The driver wasn't too good, but that was a good car."

They solemnly toasted the wrecked Dodge.

182

"To the future victories of Firebrands driven by Terry Boag," Garrett said, raising his glass again. This time Terry hesitated.

"I'm not sure I follow that," he said.

"Everybody who knows you tells me that you're really very level-headed," Garrett said. "And that you learn quick."

"Like what?"

"Like the way to make money in this business is to drive factory cars for a percentage of the prize money."

"Why the sudden interest in me? Or weren't you at the races?"

"I loathe crowds and sunshine," Garrett said. "I watched it on television. But that's not the point. The point is that you took a car driven to a certain level of performance by Red Clark, and you drove it better. The logical reason for that is that you are a better driver. And since the Firebrand hasn't done too well lately, we happen to be in the market for a better driver."

"I have the feeling this guy isn't kidding," Terry said.

"People who work for me call me Mr. Garrett," Garrett said. "I've grown used to it."

"Just like 'sir' in the army," Tony said. "You can get used to calling him Mister with a little effort."

"You better get in the habit, too, Fletcher," Garrett said.

"Not me. I'm a great believer in signs. You know, like that oracle they had at Delphi? I see a sign in my resignation from Collier, Richards & Company, and, of course, I see a sign in a certain sort of square Dodge. The oracle

183

has spoken. 'Fletcher', it says," Tony said, very solemnly, "'you don't belong in advertising and you don't belong in racing. You belong in the *trucking business.*'"

"If you're through being so very clever, Fletcher," Garrett said, "and can keep that big mouth of yours shut for ninety consecutive seconds, I have something to say."

"Shoot," Tony said.

"When I received that *dramatic* resignation of yours, I called Skeezix James to find out what horrible breach of ethics you had committed. The way that letter read, I thought you'd been caught stealing from petty cash, or carrying on with your secretary."

"Did James tell you?"

"It didn't come as a great big shock, oddly enough," Garrett said. "I knew about it all the time. I asked Red what he'd done with the Dodge, and he told me maybe twenty-four hours after he sold it to you."

"Oh," Tony said.

"So all is forgiven at Collier, Richards and Company. Your job is waiting for you. They may even roast an ox, to welcome the prodigal home."

"I appreciate whatever you said to James for me, Mr. Garrett," Tony said. "I really do. But I'm not going back there."

"Why not?"

"Things changed when I was gone, I suppose. I didn't like what I was doing."

"You mean you didn't simply love the responsibility for making all those Firebrand commercials?" Garrett was sarcastic again; Tony really never could figure him out.

184

When Tony didn't reply, Garrett said: "Tell me, Fletcher, do I have you skewered on the horse of an ethical dilemma?"

Tony didn't reply again.

"I'll have to remember whatever it was I said. This is the first time I've seen you speechless," Garrett said. "OK. I know what was going on with you and Crosby and James. Clear?"

"I still don't think I want to work there any more," Tony said.

"Good," Garrett said.

"I beg your pardon?"

"I said, 'good,'" Garrett said, "because that means if you've already made up your mind not to go back to Collier, Richards & Company, I can offer you a job without being accused of being a body stealer."

"What sort of a job?"

"Doing precisely what I wanted you to do before. That was my mistake. I realized that somewhat late. They simply couldn't put you in a position where you could tell Crosby what to do. Not with his position in the company compared to yours."

"No," Tony agreed, "they couldn't."

"But if you work for the *client*, we have what is known as a horse of a different color."

"Oh," Tony said.

"Don't get the idea that you'll be pushing Crosby around. I personally can't stand him. He reminds me of a smiling undertaker," Garrett said. "But the point is, he's good. He's experienced, and he's good. Once he gets over

185

the initial shock of having to please you with the copy, before he has to please me, he'll do a good job. He wouldn't be where he is today unless he was good. Your job will be to get him, tactfully, to see the light. Same pay, and you can work out of New York, if that makes you happy. They can find some sort of a desk for you in our New York building. You won't be around your office long enough to cause many waves, anyway."

"I don't know what to say," Tony said. He looked at Terry Boag.

"Try 'Yes, sir,' on for size," Garrett said.

"Yes, sir," the two of them said, in unison.

"That's better," Garrett said. He took out one of his long cigars and lit it. He motioned to the waitress for a menu.

Before, when Terry had said he wanted a steak, Tony had had no appetite at all. Now, suddenly, he was starving.